Touching Them All

ISBN-10: 1-4792-1200-8
EAN-13: 9781479212002
Library of Congress Control Number: 2012916210
CreateSpace Independent Publishing Platform
Noth Charleston, South Carolina

Touching Them All

Peter A. Schuller

Dedication

To my wife, Sharon, who supports me every step of the way, in whatever I am doing.

Forward

This is the first of three books that follow the journey of Charlie Howell, on his odyssey of self-discovery and investigation of what it means to be human. While the work is entirely fictional, some of the characters are based on the lives of people I have met in my own travels. More importantly, with a few exceptions, where Charlie's activities invited minor detours of speculation, all of the science represented in these three books is based on my years of research in disciplines such as neuroscience, complexity science, quantum physics, Information Theory, and genetics/epigenetics. Hopefully, the reader will embrace such science with the open-mindedness and intellectual curiosity it deserves.

What it means to be human in the 21st century obviously encompasses a wide-ranging and in many cases highly nuanced set of dynamics. For the moment, the most important thing we might do in pursuit of a deeper understanding of who we are and what we are up to is continue to ask ourselves intriguing, probing questions. Hopefully, the adventures of Charlie Howell contribute to that exercise.

In preparing to write about such adventures, I have been particularly blessed by the presence of two stimulating conversation partners, to whom I am deeply grateful—my wife, Sharon Gracen, and my good friend, Phyllis Tickle. Extraordinary women both. I am also grateful to the enthusiastic support of Jen Zehler, who read the first draft, told me it was worth publishing, and provided other important feedback.

chapter 1

CHARLIE FELT THE surge of anxiety the moment he heard the ball smacking into the catcher's mitt. He desperately hoped it was outside, but something told him it was a strike.

The umpire didn't even open his mouth, emitting a low, guttural sound while channeling most of his energy into an emphatic "punch-out" with his right arm, confirming what Charlie already knew deep in his gut. Strike three. Inning over. Game over.

Charlie Howell had committed the unpardonable sin of looking at a third strike. In the 9th inning, down a run, with a man on second. He hated the very concept—going down looking. At least when you went down swinging, you could say, well, you went down swinging. Maybe that was the reason the term caught on so easily within the American vernacular. It did seem to be a particularly American ideal, the notion that trying hard was important and that somehow trying was best manifested by doing. If you can, always take a swing at things. Take action, do something. Charlie felt that cultural ethos in his bones, and he eschewed the very idea of being passive in anything he undertook. He was a person who engaged life at every turn—if you were going down, it had to be swinging, and to add insult to injury, he just hated losing to USC.

His teammates started to gather around him, and a few tried to cheer him up.

"Charlie, don't worry about it. None of us came through today."

"Hey, you played a great game man. That was one at bat. Forget it."

"Tough call. I thought it was outside, Charlie."

"You played your heart out today, Charlie. We let *you* down."

Charlie was numbed by the thought that he had not come through when everyone was counting on him. Like many athletes, he carried a gnawing fear that he was only as good as his last performance.

"We'll get 'em next time, dude."

The chatter around him continued, but the numbness didn't lift. Every time he failed to deliver, especially in the clutch, Charlie felt like he was being exiled from the sanctuary of a world he understood, into an odyssey to ports unknown. Others seemed to experience failure differently. They accepted it and moved on. Charlie would have preferred if learning from failure was a straightforward process for him too, but it simply wasn't. He had even talked about it once with his high school baseball coach, who had immediately picked up on Charlie's attitude toward winning. From that conversation, Charlie realized it was not so much the psychological *need* to win that drove him—he just did not know any other way of projecting himself into the world than as someone who pursued, and expected, excellence; and winning was simply the most obvious way to manifest excellence. There was no excellence in looking at a called third strike.

Brian, the lanky, affable first basemen who deftly hauled in the few errant throws Charlie would occasionally make from deep in the hole at shortstop, tried to snap Charlie out of his self-absorbed state.

"Chas man, party tonight at the house. You on?"

Charlie understood that Brian knew he rarely went to parties.

"Yeah, maybe, Bri."

Charlie tuned out, deep in thought. *How had he known that pitch "sounded" like a strike? How could it be that his mind's eye had so efficiently and quickly assessed that the ball was going to be outside, commanding his entire neuromuscular system not to initiate a swing, while at the split second it hit the catcher's mitt, another system embedded deep within his brain told him almost immediately that the pitch probably was a strike after all?* Charlie was always thinking about how the brain worked and what the human mind was all about. Sometimes he even wondered why he always thought about things like that.

More than anything, though, his mind seemed to fixate on the issues of winning and failure. Supposedly the venerated football coach Vince Lombardi had once declared that "Winning isn't everything, but losing isn't anything", and that psychology had seemed to penetrate powerfully into a highly competitive American culture. Charlie didn't particularly like that philosophy, and something deep within him implicitly knew that the human person learned much more from "failure"—or, as he preferred to describe it "trial and error"—than from success. Human brains are constructed that way, Charlie kept reminding himself; they are prediction machines that process feedback and continue to make adjustments. Still, he wondered why failure on the athletic field was always so hard for him to swallow.

chapter 2

STANDING IN THE shower, steaming water pounding down on his back, Charlie's mind began to wander into that particularly intriguing space where great insights sat lurking on the edge of chaos. Regardless of what he had read from various experts in the field, he sensed one thing was true about his mental make-up—he was hard-wired to think about the mysteries of life, to wonder about the "why" questions as much as the ones involving "what" and "how".

Charlie Howell was an interesting mix. At 6'2" and 190 pounds, with sandy blond hair, a square jaw, and seemingly permanently bronzed skin, he looked every bit the southern California jock type. His wrists were thick, and his arms hung off his shoulders in a way that advertised superior agility. Most importantly, Charlie was blessed with a hidden asset, a weird quirk of genetic fate that added an unquantifiable athletic edge—he had ligaments like piano strings. It's not something that the sports scribes or scouts ever seemed to look into, but that was the secret to his edge—the special capacity some athlete's ligaments have to be repeatedly stretched to the limit of their range of motion without losing their tensile strength, especially during repeated use. In Charlie's case, it was the ligaments in his wrists that gave his bat an extra snap as it entered the strike zone, at the apex of its swing arc, and the ligaments in his shoulders that put some added zip on a throw from deep short.

But what distinguished Charlie Howell from other baseball players, what made him different, was his mind. To state that Charlie was possessed of intellectual curiosity was sort of like saying that YoYo Ma has a musical gift. Charlie not only had a sophisticated approach to the game of baseball but was majoring in neuroscience and cognitive behavior at the University of California at Irvine, known in Southern California circles simply as "UCI", though outside the state, that moniker certainly would not have been as well recognized as that of its sister school, UCLA.

Charlie was fascinated by the entire subject matter of brain function and human behavior, especially the ways in which unconscious thoughts drive behavior and how that behavior can in turn generate both conscious and unconscious thinking. For that reason, he was always surprised when told by some of the baseball scouts who had come to watch him play that for the most part major league clubs did not have their top prospects spend much time with a cognitive psychologist *before* the draft. It seemed to Charlie that in the highly competitive world of major league baseball, teams would seek out any possible advantage, including gaining better insights into whether their prospects had the mental capacity to handle the ups and downs of a major league season. Charlie supposed that clubs just figured it had become a "free agent world", in which they would not likely keep a ballplayer more than five years anyway, thereby making it less critical to perform that level of due diligence on any given draftee. Nevertheless, Charlie always wondered why any club that invested millions of dollars in scouts, draft picking methodologies, and signing bonuses would want to draft a kid who might not have the mental or physical strength to endure the marathon of a major league campaign.

Charlie's persona had another distinguishing feature—he carried an athlete's soul, the kind that instinctively took calculated risks, projected the courage of a warrior, and craved challenges. Within that soul, he carried the blessing (or, as it sometimes seemed to him, the curse) of an insatiable desire to improve. Not just his athletic skills but his mind as well. Always learning, always asking questions, always wondering how something could be done more efficiently. And he wondered about everything, from the metaphysics of creation to the hackneyed rationale his coaches always seemed to provide for bunting a runner over to second base in a close game. (Why did they always assume that a base was more valuable than an out in those situations?)

Now, as the water pounded down on his head, his perpetual mind machine was focused on something relatively mundane—why in his last at bat he had such a strong sense that the pitcher was going to throw him a curve ball on that 1-2 count, instead of the fastball that had frozen his hands on the bat. Before any answer arrived, the outside world intruded again.

"Hey, Charlie, don't sweat it, man. You look as though you just found out you've been cut from the team."

Charlie turned and saw his burly teammate Russ Moyer. *A catcher's body if there ever was one,* he noted to himself.

"I'm fine. Russ. Just lost in thought about a paper I have to write", he lied, "that's all."

"Can't fool, me, Charlie Boy. You are in one of those ways of yours. I know you."

He did. Russ was a "good old boy" from Macon, Georgia, a gregarious fellow with the kind of street smarts that allowed him to implicitly know what another person was like. Russ seemed to understand him, even though Charlie never confided in his teammates about all the things that went through his mind. It was a generally accepted truth in baseball that the less you thought about what you were doing, the better you performed. Charlie knew that his analytical mind served him more than it hindered him, because pitchers were indeed predictable, and all you had to do was spot the patterns of their behavior. But he knew that most ball players just wanted to go out there and play, not think.

Suddenly, Charlie had a thought. "Hey, Russ, you ever take any cognitive science courses?"

"Your brain must have gotten waterlogged, man. You know I don't go anywhere near science."

"Yeah, right", Charlie replied, letting a wry smile creep into the corners of his mouth, "I couldn't remember who I was talking to the other day about how the brain manages all the demands of hitting a baseball, but I guess it wasn't you."

"Got that right. But tell me what you were thinking anyway. Even the mush I have between the ears might be able to comprehend, if you don't get too technical."

"Well, you know, I was just thinking about how it was that in the 1.2 seconds it took for that last pitch to get from the pitcher's hand to the catcher's mitt, my retinas would be able to register and transmit all the data about perceived velocity, spin, and direction of the ball to the visual processing system in my cortex, and how that system was able to compare that incoming data to the data in some neural circuit where memory of other pitches—but only those from this one pitcher—were stored, formulate an assessment of what kind of pitch it was, calibrate whether it might cross the strike zone, process the decision about whether I wanted to swing at it, command dozens of muscle groups to either initiate a swing or refrain, *then* just as the ball crosses the plate go through the whole process all over again and generate a *conscious* thought that I should have swung after all!!"

Russ was transfixed. He had even stopped rubbing the shampoo into his hair and it started to cascade down his face. "Jeez, Charlie, do you really think about shit like that? And how would you possibly synthesize it into a single sentence like that one? I told you not to get technical!"

"Actually, I do think about that kind of thing a fair amount."

"How much?"

"Pretty much most of the day."

"Unbelievable. You are really unbelievable. How do you *ever* get a hit? When a guy throws you a curve, do you stand there trying to calculate the physics of its rotation?!?"

"Of course not. Not cognitively, anyway. But interesting that you mention that, because it might be precisely the answer to my question. I have heard a number of scientists speculate on how baseball players can possibly hit a 100 mph pitch or how tennis players can return a 135 mph serve, and you know what they say?"

Russ stopped his shampooing again. "No, what?"

"It can't be done. Not with the neuronal processing systems of the brain anyway."

"C'mon, Charlie, of course it's possible. We see it done every day."

"Aha, and therein lies the mystery."

The conversation had already succeeded in pulling Charlie out of his self-imposed funk, and he really wanted to engage Russ a little more on the subject. But it would have to wait. He understood how the cognitive brain gets overloaded and shuts down, and he didn't want to do that to Russ. "I tell you what, Russ, let's get out of here and go have a beer, and I will let you in on some secrets behind that mystery."

The science of it already sounded intimidating to Russ, but for some reason—maybe it was Charlie's obvious enthusiasm for the subject, he felt a little curious. "Sure, Charlie, let's do that."

chapter 3

CHARLIE WAS ALREADY half way through his Bud light, the happy hour special. "Russ, why do you play baseball?"

"Cuz it's fun."

"Yeah. Good answer. Seriously, what is special for you about the game?"

"It just seems to fit me. The skills it requires, the enjoyment I get, the satisfactions I experience, they just seem to go with who I am. I guess it makes me feel like I know myself better. I can express my true self when I play."

"Interesting. Sounds like even you have thought about this a bit. Well, OK, then, how do you know who you are, or even if you are the one playing catcher for the team?"

"C'mon, Charlie, we haven't even finished one beer. Don't go all Zen on me."

"No, seriously, what makes you think you are you, what makes you know you just said something to me I would understand?"

"Aha. I get it. You are playing mind games to make me think about what the mind is."

"Give the man an 'RBI'! You see, Russ, you are pretty clever after all. That's exactly where I was headed, and the point I want to make is that there are so many facets to the mind, so many ways of sensing consciousness about many different things, and so many takes on identity and self-perception. We really are only beginning to scratch the surface in our understanding of the human brain, mind, consciousness, and will. So in a sense, much of what it means to be human, as well as the source of our unique nature, is still a mystery."

"I see. So that's why when we were talking in the shower earlier, you said that it was a mystery how someone could possibly hit a 100 mile fastball, given how our brains are constructed."

"Well, yes, that too. I will get to that in a minute, but I am trying to impress upon you how little we know about anything really. Cosmologists and physicists think they have a good grip on the dynamics of energy and matter in our universe, but 95% of our universe is made up of dark matter and dark energy, and they don't really understand either of those phenomena yet. And even the most knowledgeable neuroscientists will confess that they only understand about 5% of the structure and functionality of the human brain. Now just given those two facts, how do you suppose we would have a good idea about what exactly is involved in the human mind and consciousness?"

"I see your point."

"Yes, so getting back to how you can hit a 100 mile an hour fastball, it is still a bit of a mystery, but I think there are some interesting possible explanations, which I would say cannot necessarily be proved at this point but also cannot be categorically ruled out."

"And what would those be? Remember, go easy on me with the technical stuff."

"Well, I don't know enough to give you a full technical explanation anyway, but there are two distinct possibilities I think. And I will try to make this as straightforward as possible."

"Thanks. And maybe I should have another beer too."

"Good idea. It will probably help me too, because it all starts off with quantum 'weirdness.' You know about quantum mechanics, right? I mean just in general terms."

"Yeah. I know that one of those famous quantum physicists once declared that if you thought you understood quantum physics you probably didn't understand the first thing about it."

"Funny. Well, there is a line of thinking that says our universe is just one big quantum computer, which constantly creates all sorts of new phenomena, by continually collapsing quantum superpositions, by way of what is called 'decoherence' or by human 'observation'."

"OK, but what does that have to do with 100 mile an hour fastballs?"

"Well, the whole idea is that if the universe is a quantum computer then so are our bodies, which means that they can process information much faster than the neural networks in our brains can, because they act more like classical analog parallel processing computers."

"I think I am lost already, Charlie."

"Not to worry. As I said, just keep the general concepts in mind. It would take me a lot more than two beers to explain it all anyway!"

"All right. And what's the other possible explanation you mentioned?"

"Well, all the energy we can observe in our little material reality here on earth basically manifests in electromagnetic waves and fields. Electromagnetic waves have different frequencies and amplitudes, which means that their many different manifestations can carry lots of different kinds of information. And when those electromagnetic waves 'interfere' with each other in such a way as to reinforce their frequency or amplitude, they can generate 'holographs' of information. When neurons in your brain fire, they also generate electromagnetic waves, which can achieve some measure of 'synchrony' across various networks and circuits, so the idea is that maybe human brains can both generate holographs of information and tap into the countless information holographs that exist within the universe."

"Totally lost me again."

"Sorry, Russ, I am doing my best."

"I am sure you are, and doubtless some of our classmates would really enjoy what you are saying. But all I know is that our brains are simple little organs that evolved over millions of years and are focused on some pretty simple tasks, like avoiding danger."

"Well, Russ, that is the truly amazing thing about the human brain, because on the one hand, you are absolutely right, but on the other, we may have a lot more going on in there than what any Darwinist or Neo-Darwinist can explain."

"What do you mean?"

"Well, let's start with this—it is true that in some respects you can hardly tell our brains apart from those of our chimp or bonobo cousins. I remember reading that researchers discovered our brains have the same basic structure and function as chimpanzees and bonobos, with whom we share about 98% of our genes, when it comes to things like identifying and cataloguing objects or reciprocating the benevolent acts of others in our same social group. But on the other hand, evolutionary biologists will tell you that by 50,000 years ago we humans had acquired slightly bigger brains, especially in the frontal cortex, than our primate cousins. Moreover, as we began to organize more sophisticated social structures 10,000 years ago, and after we invented written language 5,000 years ago, we started to adapt those bigger brains to the demands of more complex social structures. For example, when faced with the need to start cataloguing and differentiating ideas and concepts, once they could be represented in written form, the human brain simply used the same object representation and comparison system that for millions of years had been deployed to help us orient ourselves in our physical environments, except now we could connect those systems to new executive decision-making functions that developed uniquely in the human brain's neo-cortex."

"Yeah, I could see how we would have acquired a whole slew of new skills, either by adapting some existing information processing systems in the brain, or perhaps even developing new ones, but I can't see how that would make us that different from our other primates ancestors and cousins."

"It's an interesting question, Russ, and I basically agree with you. When all is said and done, there is something else to the human mind than cannot be explained by modern neuroscience or evolutionary biology. There is something else buried in the concept of consciousness that explains the extraordinary things that we do—and I am not just talking about hitting a 100 mile an hour fastball, because there are probably some pretty amazing analogues to that feat that surface throughout the animal world. No, there is something else that makes us really special, whether you call it spirit, soul, mind, or whatever. And the most fascinating part about it is that somehow, this evolved organ we call the human brain is precisely the complex adaptive system that either gives rise to this emergent phenomenon of human spirit or else serves in some way as the mechanism for its expression within the human mind. It's why I am so passionate about studying neuroscience."

"Well, I doubt that you will figure it out before the end of the season, Charlie, but I hope that doesn't prevent you from swinging away at those 100 mile an hour fastballs, rare as they may be!"

"Not to worry. I can shut down my conscious mind and focus as well as the next guy when I have to. But speaking of neuroscience, I had better get about to studying for that test tomorrow!! Thanks for the beer, Russ. It was fun."

"My pleasure. And good luck on the test."

"Thanks."

chapter 4

CHARLIE HAD NOT seen Sarah in two days, and when he had spotted her crossing the Campus Drive pedestrian overpass, a flood of thoughts and feelings rushed into his consciousness. *Sarah Wilson. What was it about her that he found so interesting? Why was he so attracted to her? Was it physical, emotional, or something else?* He had never been so fascinated by anyone in his life. *And why hadn't he asked her out yet?*

From the moment they met three months ago, after she had answered an ad he had posted online to unload his old Apple iBook, Charlie had been captivated by her presence. She was undoubtedly beautiful. Tall and slender, with a tint of red in her light auburn hair, and sparkling green eyes, Sarah was what Charlie called "striking". She was a music major with an enchanting mezzo soprano voice and a soft touch on the piano. But for Charlie, the most fascinating aspect of Sarah Wilson was her clever mind, and the way she used it to carry herself. He simply enjoyed her company, and they enjoyed meeting occasionally for lunch. Charlie just was not sure he wanted to change any of the dynamics of their relationship by asking her out, and Sarah seemed equally pleased with the current state of affairs.

He hurried his step, accelerated briefly into a short sprint, then slowed as he came within earshot. *Never want to seem too eager.*

"Sarah", he called out, rather more expectantly than he would have preferred.

She turned quickly, a smile of recognition crossing her face. "Hey, Charlie, how are you?"

"Just great. You?"

"Brilliant."

Charlie was temporarily distracted. He knew Sarah had picked up the expression during her summer study in London the year before, but he sort of wished she had dropped the rather overused British manner of speech by now.

"Where are you headed?"

"To my voice lesson. You?"

"On my way to class too. Neuroscience test."

"Lucky you. What's the test on?"

"First few chapters. Just general structure and function of the brain. Nothing that would make for great conversation, I am afraid."

Sarah looked a little disappointed, so Charlie tried a quick recovery. "You know me, I always love a good conversation, so any time you want…."

"Well, actually, I am not sure I really do know you, Charlie, but I know enough to be confident that you are a fun conversation partner, and I always learn something when I talk with you."

Charlie tried on his best Humphrey Bogart. "Stick around kid, and there's no telling what you might learn." He thought the accent worked well enough that Sarah would recognize what he was up to and think it was funny, not presumptuous.

"I might just do that. Well, it it's good to see, you, Charlie. I got to get going."

Charlie's mind was instantly trying to gauge the motivation or desire behind Sarah's response. "Yeah, good to run into you too, Sarah."

As they turned and started to take their separate ways, Sarah glanced back over her shoulder and casually called back, "Charlie, how about lunch today?"

"Sure, great. Wonderful. I would love to." Already he was regretting how eager he sounded. "When and where?"

"How about In and Out Burger at 12:30?"

"Works for me. See you then."

Charlie sensed immediately a small bounce in his step and a quick burst of some deep-seated emotion he thought must be something like hope or just some form of inchoate optimism. *There is something about that girl.*

chapter 5

By the time each of them had finished their burgers and turned their attention to a basket of fries they were jointly pulling on, Charlie had discovered what was so intriguing to him about Sarah Wilson. She was unquestionably handsome, a statuesque figure whose movements announced her confident and cheerful nature every time she entered a room. But there was something else too, a more mysterious quality that immediately attracted her to others, especially men.

As Sarah told him about growing up in Amman, Jordan, where her father had served as Cultural Attaché in the U.S. Embassy, Charlie began to get a keen sense of her restless, mercurial, and highly curious personality. She clearly enjoyed the high levels of cultural stimulation that had defined her early environment, which apparently had made her very comfortable with, even oriented toward, the exotic and the unconventional. As Sarah plunged further into the history of her upbringing and the lives of her parents, Charlie also surmised that she was a product of the highly intentional manner in which her parents had modeled an engaging life for their children's benefit.

When he asked her about this, Sarah explained that she had been particularly impressed with how much her parents always seemed to be living in a sense of abundance, eager to find the delight, the challenge, or the opportunity to learn a valuable life lesson from whatever circumstances confronted them at any given moment. They had very clearly emphasized to her that adversity is not only a great opportunity to build character but to reveal it as well. And they had made sure she would cherish her past but not be ruled by it.

"It was their transparency," Sarah had finally said to him, as she honed in on what really distinguished her parents in her mind. "I always remember their referring to the idea of transparency and how humans can learn to get out of their own way so they can see themselves and others better for who they really are in their heart of hearts, where dreams seek to touch down in reality. They were constantly asking each other questions, and when the three of us kids were old enough, they started in on us too!"

Sarah was the middle of the three children and had clearly learned to play the intermediary's role with aplomb. She was articulate, graceful, and comfortable with a wide range of personalities. She listened well, could understand different points of view with great facility, was a good integrator, and seemed good at solving problems. In the thirty minutes that they had been exchanging stories of their childhood experiences, Charlie had already seen evidence of all those characteristics.

The more she talked, the more captivated Charlie became, and soon he was firing his questions. "So what kind of things did you talk about with your parents? Did they spend a lot of one on one time with you or were you together as family every day? Did you have great conversations at dinner? Did—"

"Hey, Charlie, slow down. One at a time. Man, are you always like this? You're as bad as my parents!"

"I bet you can keep up. C'mon. Answers, I want answers." Charlie stopped, wondering if he was sounding a bit demanding, or perhaps too familiar. Sarah's smile assured him otherwise.

"You're right. I can keep up. Yes to all. Next question."

"Very funny."

"I mean it. My dad, Frank, had lots of official functions he had to attend, but he always made sure we had one meal together as a family every day, even if it was breakfast. And he would quiz us about all sorts of topics—especially world affairs. You had to be up on your world affairs if you were going to be an active member of the Wilson family."

"And I would walk the souk—that's the indigenous marketplace—in downtown Amman with my mom practically every Saturday morning, and we would talk about everything from King Hussein's place in Arab history to what I wanted to do when I grew up. Sometimes my dad and I would go riding on a Sunday afternoon, find a nice quiet place in the outskirts of town, and just

sit under some fig trees and talk. He was the most fascinating man I have ever known."

Charlie had not had much experience at dating,
but he had seen a movie once that dealt with the difficult issues of marriage and relationship, and he remembered that the big problem in the story had centered
around the husband's inability to measure up to his
wife's vision of what her husband would be like, because she had so adored her father. He guessed that
Sarah might have been a candidate for that trap but
that she would somehow be clever enough to avoid it.

"That does sound awesome. My dad died when I
was six, so I missed out on all that."

"I'm sorry, Charlie. That must have been hard."

"Harder on my mom than me, but yeah, I really
miss him."

"I am sure you do. What do you remember about
him?"

"Well, I don't remember that much, but I just loved
being around him, and later I did hear a lot about him.
He had played for 5 years in the Cubs organization, but
only one September at the Friendly Confines—that's
Wrigley Field—in 1980. He quit the next year when he
did not make the team coming out of spring training.
He was tired of the travel and wanted to be with me
and mom. I was 2. He got a job as a sportswriter for the
Washington Post. Four years later, he died from a brain
tumor."

"Sorry."

"Thanks. I am reconciled to it now. And there are certain things about him I carry with me all the time, like his love of baseball."

"Yeah, I heard you are pretty good."

"Who told you?"

"Good journalists and coy females never reveal their sources."

"Which are you?"

Sarah smiled coyly and moved on. "So is it true, are you a good player?"

"I see what you're doing. You must be a good journalist, or a salesperson in the making. Always asking questions to avoid getting pinned down yourself."

"Busted. Now answer the question."

"Yes, I am pretty good. There might even be some baseball in my future after graduation."

"Cool. Scouts been calling?"

"Nothing gets by you, huh? Yeah, in fact a Red Sox scout called me three days ago and said they were thinking about taking me in an early round this year. Of course, that was before I took a third strike to end the USC game the other day."

"Heard about that one too."

"Interesting. Are you stalking me?"

"Just a curious reporter gathering information for a story."

"Whose story?"

"I'm taking the Fifth on that one."

"Good journalist *and* coy female."

"Busted again."

Charlie shifted restlessly in his chair. He knew he was running out of time and did not want the conversation to end quite yet. The moment would be lost if they tried to pick up the thread at a later date. And he sensed that a connection was starting to develop between them. "Sarah, what was the most important thing your parents conveyed to you?"

"Well, in addition to making sure we never got trapped in the past, they really drummed into us how critical it was to live in the present."

"What's the difference?"

"I thought you might ask. At first, I did not really get it either, but my parents were good about explaining things, especially with reference to their own experience. Basically what they meant was that unless we are careful, we all tend to get stuck in illusory worlds that are of our own making and which don't necessarily reflect what is actually going on around us."

"You mean we all have our own perceptions of reality, so there really is no Reality with a capital "R"?"

"No, that is more metaphysical than the concept I was referring to. What my parents meant, and I have noticed over the last several years that it is true, is that we have so much stuff, so many stories, running through our consciousness that we are not accurately registering what is going on in front of our faces. We hear a certain tone of voice, a word, or see an image, and it sends us off into some embedded memory, a long held dream, or just some mundane illusion we live in without even knowing it. It's all pretty natural, given the way we are put together, but it costs us something to live like that."

"I see."

"Someday, when we have a little more time, I will tell you more about what my parents learned—and believe me they had to learn it just like anyone would, because it is not the natural way for us to be—about listening generatively into life, so you don't get lost in its many illusions and end up some day looking back and saying, 'wow, that was somebody else's life I lived for 40 years, too bad it took me so long to wake up to what *my* life is supposed to be about'".

"Yeah, I would love to hear more, but it sounds like it would take a while. And shoot, look what time it is. I have class in 15 minutes, a quiz in fact, so I cannot be late."

"Oh, you're right. I have to run too.

"It was fun. Thank you, Sarah. Thanks for the invitation."

"You are most welcome. I really enjoyed it too." Sarah gave a quick wink. "Besides, I was getting tired of stalking you from a distance and decided it would be safe to move in a little closer."

Charlie chuckled softly. *Did she mean that seriously? Maybe I have been missing something.* "Catch you later, Sarah."

"You too, Charlie. And if I don't see you before then, good luck against UCLA."

"Thanks. Hey, Sarah. What's your email address?"

"It's sawilson@uci.edu."

"Thanks. I'll drop you a note later. A couple of things I thought of when you were talking earlier. Hey, what does the "a" stand for?"

"Not on a first date. A girl has to have some secrets, you know."

Charlie gave a quick smile in response. *"First date"? Yeah, something has definitely changed.*

chapter 6

CHARLIE SUDDENLY NOTICED he was biting his lip pretty hard. The exam question was not particularly difficult, and he was well prepared for it. Charlie always found it a bit strange that he got nervous during exams, no matter how well prepared he was. It was one of the many intriguing aspects of his behavior, one that he imagined he shared with quite of number of other people, which had intrigued him so much as a youth and prompted him to take up the study of neuroscience in college. He took a deep breath and read the question again.

"Question I. 20 points. Explain the term "working memory" and its role in formulating human consciousness."

After a few minutes of jotting down terms and sketching a short outline, Charlie started in.

The term 'working memory' is used to describe the management system used by the brain to generate and process incoming stimuli, thoughts and feelings, among the many competing systems of the brain. Thought to employ neural circuits and networks located in the fron-

tal cortex of the brain, working memory's functions include comparing and contrasting sensory stimuli with existing long term memories, in order to formulate a set of intentions for action, register commands for the actions themselves, and predict the possible consequences of such actions. Recent research suggests that memories are stored in different parts of the brain and can be activated by many different types of emotional or sensory stimuli. When memories are activated in this manner, through the synaptic firings that connect various neurological circuits and systems, they are processed and managed in 'working memory' and experienced as thoughts and feelings. In this vein, working memory becomes a form of "central processor" where long term memories can be revisited and reprocessed. Human consciousness relies on the existence of memories to provide orientation and context, which are essential to the unity of consciousness humans experience when they are awake and orientating themselves within their environments.

Because working memory, which can be defined as memory x processing, *necessarily involves conscious "attention" to sensory stimuli, it plays a critical role in several aspects of human consciousness. Recurring feedforward and feedback processing that takes place in working memory also provides a platform from which self-reflective human consciousness emerges. In other words, we can only become aware that we are aware of our surroundings and responses to them by and through the processes of working memory. There are of course many other aspects of human consciousness, but working memory is the essential brain system that determines whether the brain generates a "conscious" experience or simply registers information to be processed later in the "unconscious" areas of the brain, which can also ultimately affect a person's consciousness.*

Charlie stopped typing on his laptop and looked at the rest of the exam, which seemed straightforward enough. He was fascinated by neuroscience and easily distracted by different ideas and thoughts that came rushing in from time to time. Indeed, he decided to add the last paragraph of his answer, even though there was no substantial scientific work to support his hypothesis. It just seemed to be the way his mind worked. Always branching out in search of new ideas. His mind began to wonder, thinking of Socrates's famous philosophy, *the unexamined life is not worth living.*

But just as quickly, his own working memory started processing an old mental tape of a test he took in 9th grade that he had failed miserably, because he had run out of time, having spent too long on an essay question that had captivated him. The memory of that moment stabbed him with the sharp edge of fear, and he refocused his attention back to the exam paper. Funny how the brain works, Charlie mused as he began to bring himself out of the grip of fear—it never seems to stop connecting emotions, thoughts, and feelings in seemingly random ways. Of course, he knew it really was not random at all. He knew how sensory stimuli activated neural networks and set about retrieving memories filed deep within the different parts of the brain's cortices. He knew perfectly well that the brain stores memories not as a collection of hard data but as an interpreted experience, and that each interpretation always had some emotional component to it. *One day we will understand it all,* Charlie imagined. *Or maybe not.* He rather embraced the mystery of it all too.

Within the hour, he was finished with the midterm for his Cognitive Behavior 201 course and with a quick "drag and drop" of the mouse deposited his answers into the professor's electronic in-box.

chapter 7

HE AWOKE IN his usual existential cloud, the one that made him feel he had to spend a few hours reorienting his consciousness. It was hard for Charlie to describe what it felt like inside that cloud. He had tried to explain it to his mother once—it only happened when he first got up, but it could last for several hours. Not exactly a dread, feeling of desperation, or incapacity of any sort. More like a vague sensation that something was not right, a consciousness that contained no specific thoughts but clearly conveyed that something was off—it had an inchoate quality of hopelessness that made no sense to Charlie, whose future looked pretty bright in virtually every respect. It was as if while he slept his soul journeyed to a dimension outside time and space, then had to make some forced reentry back into the realities of earthly life, where synching up again with a conscious ego generated a deep and unsettling perturbation that defied description in terms of a specific thought, emotion, or feeling.

Because Charlie's father had died so young, it was up to his mother, who worked long hours teaching French and German to high school students in Potomac, Maryland, to help Charlie deal with these experiences. Feeling out of her element, she had sent him to a psychiatrist, who had diagnosed the condition as inadequate levels of serotonin and had tried several different types of medication, but Charlie soon tired of the routine and claimed that nothing really took the cloud away. Charlie discovered that the best way to deal with the condition was simply to engage as soon as possible in some form of physical activity, which seemed to generate either the necessary endorphins or mental distractions that somehow helped to reboot his computer and reset his consciousness. Sometimes a good conversation could do the same thing, and today it was his roommate, Nate Cleary, who came to the rescue.

"Hey, Chas, I need your help with something."

"Sure, no sweat. What's the story?"

"You are into all that mind stuff, right?"

"Yeah. What exactly are you talking about?"

"Well, the stuff about what the human mind is, how it works, that sort of thing."

Nate was a bright guy, who had transferred to UCI from UCSD to study computer programming, but the question surprised Charlie. In all the conversations he had ever had with Nate, they had never talked about anything metaphysical.

"Well, yeah, Nate, I am studying that in our Cognitive Behavior course, but what exactly do you need help with?"

"How I am supposed to get my mind around death."

Charlie sat up straight and unconsciously brushed his hair, starting to focus his mind more acutely and sensing the usual rush of anticipation that he always seemed to have when someone asked him an intriguing question. Because of what he had learned in the classroom and the long hours of conversation with his mother, he had come to the realization that he was one of those people who liked to know things just so that he could respond to anyone who had big questions about life, or death. And while he loved to be responsive to others, especially when they were asking metaphysical questions, he also invariably felt a tinge of pressure—Charlie took life and its meaning very seriously.

"Wow, Nate, that's kind of big question. Tell me why that came up and what you think about it now."

"I grew up in the Catholic Church and I believe in God and everything, but all of a sudden the other day, I started getting this huge, overwhelming sense of fear about death. I tried sorting it out in my mind—you know, working it out rationally—but I couldn't come up with anything that put me at ease. So I figured that maybe you could help me understand more about what happens in my mind and what fear is all about, cognitively.

"Interesting. Very interesting. Yeah, I think I can help. Let's go down to Starbucks and talk about it. I don't have class till 11. What about you?"

"Yeah, I'm cool."

chapter 8

THE UCI CAMPUS, being only four miles from the Pacific coast, was still blanketed by a heavy bank of clouds, known locally as the "marine layer", which would eventually burn off. Charlie often thought that the marine layer in Southern California was like the existential cloud he awoke to almost every morning. It was grey and formless, but as the day wore on, it invariably lifted and gave way to radiant sunshine. It was often that way for Charlie's moods as well.

Nate and Charlie decided to grab their coffee and sit outside where the ambient air was wet and serene, which seem to pull Charlie into an even more pensive state. Nate decided to jump right in.

"So, Charlie, what are you afraid of?"

"Striking out with the bases loaded."

"Seriously."

"I am being serious."

"That's it?"

"Well, not exactly. I guess you could say I am afraid of failure in any type of performance."

"Why do you think that is?"

"Not sure exactly. Probably something to do with not wanting to disappoint my mother. My dad died when I was six, and I was all she had, so I always wanted to please her, make her proud of me. Guess I probably thought it would somehow make my dad proud of me too."

"So you think your dad *knows* what is going on in your life now?"

"Well, I suppose that is kind of a figure of speech, isn't it? I mean, I sense that he has some connection still with my mom and me, but I couldn't tell you exactly how. I am better at understanding the workings of the brain than grasping spiritual or religious truths. I have read a few things about the human 'soul', but I don't really understand it. In fact, my spirituality and religious beliefs are pretty undeveloped right now. Of course, I have some scientific based notions about how it all might work, but they are a bit emergent too, so I don't think they would help us here."

"But when I brought up my fear of death earlier, you didn't sound like you had any yourself. You sounded pretty calm and collected about the whole thing."

"Probably mostly because I have not thought about it much lately—I wouldn't say that I am comfortable with the whole idea that some day I will die. Once I understood exactly what it meant that my father had died, I did think about it a lot, but eventually I just let it go. Still, it's not like I am sanguine about death, and I don't really know what I believe about God or the concept of eternal life."

"Oh. Well, what are your thoughts about *my* fear?"

"Tell me more about it. When does it grab you, Nate? How does it manifest itself?"

"It can happen at any time really. I suppose it happens more often when I start thinking about the big questions of life. I took a Western philosophy class last year, and I guess that got me to thinking about what the purpose of life is and why I am here. When I think about what my life means, it occurs to me that it will be over in another 60 or 70 years, and that's when I start getting these overwhelming feelings of fear—fear of just no longer being around—being non-existent—is the best way I can describe it."

"Well, I would guess what you are sensing is pretty normal. The brain is geared to experiencing fear, and it's also designed to be in control. In many respects, the brain is responsible for the proper functioning of the entire body, not to mention being charged with orienting the human person in the world and in society. So, understandably, the brain does not naturally generate thoughts of its non-existence. I am sure that's why we experience what we call the phenomenon of ego, which also is fearful and likes to be in control. Systems analysts would call the ego an emergent property of the brain, and the part of your consciousness that senses the desire to exist would be another emergent property of the brain. If that is the case, it would be easy to understand why your mind would have a fear of non-existence, and occasionally that fear bubbles to the surface and into your consciousness."

41

"That sounds so simple, Charlie. And so difficult to avoid."

"Well, I suppose that is true. You know, I have read how some philosophers and theologians say that fear of death is archetypal, but to my way of thinking it simply results from the nature of our brains. Our brains are self-organizing systems that are geared toward one primary goal, survival. But in the case of humans, survival now means a lot more than just avoiding being eaten by a tiger on the savannah. So now our brains have many sub-systems that work together to make sure not only that the body operates properly but that we develop a sense of identity, learn how to promote and protect that identity in society, and all sorts of other survival functions. These brain systems generate the awareness we humans carry of our own existence—both a blessing and a curse I suppose. We are burdened with the knowledge that we are alive, that our bodies will degenerate over time, and that therefore we will—at least in physical form—cease to exist at some time in the future. Of course that's an unsettling notion!"

Nate smiled uncomfortably. Charlie noticed, hesitated, then continued. "You can see how in many cases fear might simply be an emergent property that alerts you to a real and present danger, perhaps even saves your life, while in other cases it may just be an illusion, something that just emerges from the many thoughts, emotions, and feelings that are always circulating in your unconscious mind. So one of the great challenges of life is managing our ubiquitous fears, paying attention to the ones that help us survive and letting go of the ones that are mere illusions of a self-organizing brain and a fertile mind. Unfortunately, we are not consciously aware of so much that goes on in our brains and minds that it can be difficult to manage the illusory fears once they have taken root in our unconscious minds."

"That's really interesting, Charlie."

"Well, actually, it just got me to thinking I should explain the whole picture of thoughts, emotions, and feelings—what they really are in terms of how the brain works. You up for that?"

"Yeah, sure."

"I will try to make this as simple and straightforward as I can. The first thing to appreciate is that basically all our experiences of life are subjective, whether you are talking about thoughts, emotions, or expressions of will, primarily because each of us has a uniquely formed brain and each of us encounters our own chain of experiences as we grow up."

"As you may know, every person's DNA contains a unique set of instructions that allows different genes in different kinds of cells to turn other genes on and off, in order to manufacture essential proteins for building new cells, sending information to other cells, and all sorts of complex transactions that define molecular biology. Since the human genome was mapped a few years ago, biologists continue to discover new insights into the complex world of gene expression, but suffice it to say that precisely how a person's brain develops, and how all of properties of mind that emerge from the brain's functioning manifest, depend on not only the structural and functional preferences mapped out *in utero* but the complex interplay between that person's genome and the physical environment, events, and experiences that person undergoes throughout her life. With me?"

"Sort of, Charlie. But go on."

"As our brains develop *in utero*, they first create over 100 billion neurons, then after birth, they create another 100 billion, though after a year or so about half of the 200 billion die off, because they are not used enough. On top of that, there are another trillion glial and other support cells, which may also have some effect on the brain's initial structure, future development, and functional versatility. In the entire brain building process, which goes on for 25 years, a certain amount of random development occurs, for reasons ranging from the biochemistry of your mother's womb to the physical stimuli your brain encounters, in the structure and potential "wiring" of the billions of synapses that are critical for all the brain's normal operation."

Nate was struggling to keep up, but his facial expressions indicated he was paying attention, so Charlie continued.

"Moreover, it is a well accepted theory now that our brains actually continue to create neurons throughout our lifetimes—the harder you work your brain the more it grows, and increasingly it reflects the set of environmental factors that bear down upon it. So our brains are always changing, just based on how we experience life, and this obviously gives us all completely unique minds, experiences of consciousness, ways of perceiving the world, and inclinations toward certain types of behavior."

Nate looked confused. "OK, but what does that have to do with my fear of death?"

"Sorry. I am coming to that. Anyway, eventually in this drawn out process that makes our brains and minds unique, our brains also become highly efficient information processors, which means they favor the use of particular systems of neurons that have wired together from regular use. For example, as you learn to ride a bike, the different sets of visual perception, motor control, and executive function systems that must be wired together through a complex series of synaptic connections in order to result in the coordinated movement of all your muscles, all those dedicated sets of neurological networks 'fire together' and, after much repetition, then get 'wired together'. If the activity becomes sufficiently rote, as would be the case with riding a bike after a few months, the entire activity, represented in a neural network, can be relegated to a sub-cortical region of the brain so that it remains dedicated to a specific function and cannot be highjacked by other functions. In essence, they fall into the category of what is commonly known as 'muscle memory' in the case of physical talents and 'unconscious or subconscious behavior' in the case of interpersonal or social activities. In the case of less rote activities, like driving a car, some aspects of the process may be relegated to sub-cortical regions while others, like adjusting to icy road conditions, would not be, since they require constant learning and relearning, as well as the conscious adaptation to changing conditions."

Nate nodded, indicating his understanding.

"These neural networks serve as the building blocks for the brain's memory system and the mind's ability to perform various functions, like orienting itself in time and space, recognizing patterns, and making comparative judgments about those patterns. Essentially, to perform these functions, the brain establishes millions of connectors among synaptic circuits within different parts of the brain and builds complex systems, generating what we categorize as thought, emotion, or will. The key here is to understand that all of these systems are integrated—in other words, you can never have a thought that is not in some way, however minor or *unconscious,* connected to an emotion, because the brain's system for processing emotion is completely integrated with all other memory and cognitive thinking systems."

"Give me an example."

"Right. When you look at my face as I am speaking, there are billions of synaptic events going on in your brain, as the cones and rods in the back of your retina are bombarded by photons and begin to translate that data into signals that are transmitted from the retinal nerve to different parts of your visual cortex, the parts of your brain that organize and process that data into images and percepts. Of course, at the same time, a parallel process is going on in your auditory system, and much of that separately processed information is eventually integrated, in the part of your brain that is used as a central processor—called working memory— with the output from your visual system. Not only that, but all that data then gets integrated with memories related to the stimuli each system is processing—maybe certain words I use or facial expressions that emerge as I am speaking—gets connected to some memory or otherwise precipitates some emotional response in your brain. Perhaps the tone of my voice sounds like your father's, or some part of my face reminds you of your brother's, and whether you are aware of it or not, your brain could be connecting something I say with a stern lecture you got from one of them and attaching the tone of my voice to the emotions you experienced during that lecture."

Nate's eyes suddenly brightened. "So, Charlie, do you mean to say that if all of a sudden, I spilled this hot coffee on my lap, I might get some huge rush of fear, because my brain immediately associates the event with a time when I was five and my older sister accidentally poured boiling water on my leg and burned it?"

"That is quick, Nate, and yes, that is precisely what I was suggesting. Of course, the situation you describe is a rather limited one, which most of us will never have to face, so it does not necessarily help us understand the more amorphous fears that we seem to dwell on, like your fear of death. Anyway, the key thing I wanted to convey is that emotions are real, concrete, biochemical phenomena that are generated in the brain and the whole body, through processes that you will not always be conscious of and which therefore may create thoughts and feelings in you that you don't understand."

"So you are saying that my fear of death might be coming out of my unconscious mind? How would I ever get to the bottom of that? It sounds like I need a shrink.'"

"Relax. As I said earlier, this is all quite normal. And no, there is nothing you can do about all the stuff being processed in your unconscious mind. It's just a reality of human life. The human brain is able to process over 400 million of bits of information a second, but working memory—the central processor if you will—can only absorb about 2500 bits a second. So you see, there is a lot that escapes what neuroscience refers to as 'access consciousness', or what we would commonly call our 'conscious awareness'."

Nate smiled knowingly. Finally, they were touching a subject he understood. "So you might say by analogy that a computer's CPU has consciousness of whatever data it happens to be processing at any given moment in RAM but not everything that is stored within its ROM."

"Well, I am sure that is what you computer types would love to believe, and what some philosophers like to contemplate when they discuss robots and Artificial Intelligence, but the fact of the matter is that the brain is not really like a computer. It's a parallel *analogue* processor that operates more by association and pattern recognition than by processing digital bytes of 1's and 0's. But most importantly, the human brain generates incredible rich and complex emergent phenomena, like feelings, motivation, personality, and even some aspects of consciousness. Computers cannot create phenomenal consciousness—stuff like generative thoughts and feelings. They are not able to tell you that they are aware of exactly what information they are processing, what the consequence of their output might be, or how that will make them "feel". They are not able to describe a dynamic "experience", or to reflect on the morality of what they are doing, or countless other such functions."

"Well, that sounds like an interesting discussion in and of itself. But getting back to your example, what else is going on in my brain that generates a consciousness, as you call it, about what my eyes are focused on or what my ears are hearing?"

"Nate, I think in many ways it comes down to information feedback loops of one kind or another. Feedback loops in the brain are essential for maintaining the body's homeostasis—you know, like keeping your body's temperature at 98.6 degrees. But feedback loops are also important in retaining your focus and attention, or even making judgments. For example, the way 'working memory' associates stored emotional data to incoming visual data and feeds it back into the brain's executive functions in the neo-cortex is a critical component of being able to anticipate the consequences of one's actions and make a judgment about what to do in a given situation."

"So if that is true, the many feedback loops in the brain must also be able to generate some powerful illusions, because as any philosopher or computer programmer knows, output is always affected by initial conditions or premises."

"Right again, Nate. That's precisely what happens, and to make matters even more insidious, the brain does not distinguish between incoming information and stored information, because it's all processed the same way—a synaptic connection or neural network of connections. So, if your unconscious mind generates some wild notion that escapes into a natural feedback loop, it can generate—and continue to reinforce—some very dangerous illusions. It's probably what accounts for sociopathic behavior and political ideology like fascism."

"So what you are saying Charlie is that my fear of death might be connected to some incident that took place in my early life that made me very afraid or which I somehow associated with the end of life as I understood it at the time and which now may be embedded in some unconscious feedback loop?"

"I suppose that could be, Nate. There are all sorts of possible explanations for what resides in your consciousness and how it got there, and I am just giving you a neuroscientific viewpoint, and a rough estimate at that. Science is most useful when it works in collaboration with philosophy and theology, because science can help answer the 'how' questions while philosophy and religion are better at the 'why' questions. There may be all sorts of karmic or other types of 'realities' that bear on human consciousness generally, and your fear of death specifically. The point I want to make is that emotions are fundamental to the human experience, and they accumulate over the years, embedding themselves within the neurological system of the entire body, not just the brain; those emotions are constantly feeding information back into the brain's various processing systems and engendering all sorts of thoughts and feelings. It takes a great deal of work to sort out the cause and effect relationships between all those unconscious thoughts, emotions, and feelings, in terms of what we cognitively process."

"I think I get the picture. So what you are really saying is that my fear may be perfectly normal, and I can't really be sure what prompts it, but there might be something I could *consciously* do to avoid—or maybe I should say 'short circuit' it."

"Clever, Nate, I underestimated you. Or maybe you underestimate yourself."

"Thanks, I think, but I am not sure I know what to do to consciously alter my sense of fear."

"Understandable. Most people don't like to think that there is so much more going on inside their brains and minds than they can control, or even be consciously aware of enough to control. We are fearful creatures, because we are sensitive creatures—according to complexity science, the more complex a system is, the more sensitive it is to the conditions of its environment, and clearly there is no more complex system in the world than the human being. Frankly, it seems to me your fear of death is healthy, perhaps even a sign of a very efficient brain, but that probably does not make it any more fun to live with. Death is simply a part of life, and if we choose to distract ourselves from that reality, I don't know that we are doing ourselves any favors."

"So what DO *I* do?"

"Well, the most powerful tool in dealing with any issue is gaining awareness of it, what it brings up in terms of emotions and feelings. If you do that, you may be able to let go of what you find unpleasant and counterproductive in your life. Sometimes in letting go of something, it helps to talk about it, so I am glad you came to me."

"OK…"

"And remember, the way memories get stored in the brain's neural circuitry, the more you think about something and attach powerful feelings to it, the "stronger" the memory becomes. The synaptic connections representing those memories are ready to fire with abandon when any external stimulus comes along to engage them. So the more you choose to think about death, the more likely you are to keep regenerating those fears."

"So let me see if I get this, Charlie. If I just let the fear come up and let it hang around, without getting upset about it, thinking about the implications of death and what not, the more likely I can actually let go of it, if I choose to?"

"Sounds right to me. As I said, I am no expert."

"Well I guess you gave me the good news and the bad news. The good news is that what I am sensing is a pretty normal fear, and the bad news is that it takes a lot of hard work to overcome it. Anyway, thanks for sharing all that. One thing is for sure, you are one hell of a smart dude."

"Thanks, Nate. I consider that a great compliment, but I doubt if smarts necessarily helps one figure out how to deal with one's fears. Now, I gotta run to class. How about you?"

"I have some time. I think I am just going to sit here for a bit and think about some things." Nate started to chuckle. "From now on, I am going to be seeing those little circuits in my brain forming and reforming as I sit and contemplate something. I hope I don't drive myself nuts!"

"Not to worry, my man. Our minds couldn't keep up with that level of multi-level processing. You might be able to do it for a few minutes, but eventually your brain would just get tired and start shoving aside all the useless functions like thinking about what you are thinking about!! Trust me, I have done it myself more than once."

"Spoken like a true guru, my friend."

chapter 9

Philosophy and Social Order 302 was just beginning when Charlie slipped in the back door of the lecture hall. Apart from Neurophysiology of the Brain, this was his favorite course. Today's lecture involved the neurophysiology of the brain as an organ of social facilitation—what some neuroscientists were starting to call the human "social brain". Fortunately, Charlie had read the professor's latest book, which investigated the hypothesis that because humans are highly social animals their brains must have evolved some unique functionality and physiology. Charlie settled into his seat, suddenly thinking about Sarah and wondering if he might learn something about the brain's approach physical attraction.

Professor Kolowski jumped right into the topic.

"One big problem that philosophy has with neuroscience concerns the gap between the known cumulative effect of brain mechanics and the manifestation of human behavior in society. Nothing in neuroscience adequately explains how humans develop a social consciousness and a moral conscience from the cumulative effect of neural activity. The only way to explain such social phenomena is by way of 'emergence', which we will get to in more detail later. At least in most philosophical circles, it is generally accepted that the neurobiology of the brain is not sufficient alone to explain the full breadth of human sentient experience. And even assuming that the human mind is supervenient upon—meaning that it is dependent on but not completely defined by the physiology of—the brain, we still have to deal with the nature and origin of human will. For example, what do we know about the correlation between free will and Hebbian plasticity? You remember Hebbian learning, right—the tendency of neural networks that share common characteristics, proximity, or information processing function to wire together?"

"Good. So that brings us to this question—what are the neurological implications of what we might call conscious intentions and how do they relate to the thoughts we have regarding what we experience as the manifestation of "will"? For the most part, science seems only to have proved that the conscious thought you have when you *sense* you have caused an action to take place may actually take place *after* the synaptic processes laid out in the brain to orchestrate such action have already been set in motion! As you know from your readings, Benjamin Libet did a number of experiments to support this theory."

"All this is to say that apparently, because of our constant interaction with the environment around us, including our social contacts, our brains are wired to make us implicitly social beings, able to produce a number of conscious and unconscious social behaviors that are in part engendered by the social circumstances and environment we find ourselves in—or, to put it another way, human will is a function of its situational environment. But where do the impetuses for such social behaviors come from we might ask?"

Charlie loved this type of metaphysical quandary but was finding it difficult to concentrate. Sarah Wilson was occupying both his working memory and his consciousness. He tried to tune his attention back into the professor's voice.

"Of course, as I suggested earlier, we always have the concept of emergent properties to explain some of these phenomena. As you all know, the brain and body together make up a very complex, adaptive neurological and biochemical system, by integrating a number of quite complex sub-systems, such as the autonomous nervous system, the system of organs and glands that produce all the hormones, peptides, and amines that build the neurotransmitters which are critical to the brain's functioning, and so forth. And as we all know from systems thinking generally, every complex adaptive system generates emergent properties and phenomena, which then have the capacity to causally alter the structure and dynamics of the system from which they emerge. Our brains manage to generate the emergent phenomena of ambition and will, and by the exercise of that will, the thoughts, behaviors, and even structures of our brain can be changed. So it could be that some of the phenomena we will discuss in this class, such as the origin of social consciousness and will, are simply contained in the yet unidentified emergent properties of the system that makes up the entirety of the human mind."

Charlie rarely went an entire lecture without asking a question. Again, he found he could not help himself and raised his hand.

"Professor, how do we become social beings at all? Is that an emergent property, of a larger system—let's call it society—formed when a number of people organize themselves into a community?"

"Excellent question, Mr. Howell. What do you think?"

"Well, I guess that makes as much sense to me as anything. The brain is obviously always processing information and monitoring feedback—you know, like the system that regulates body temperature, organ functions, etc.—so why wouldn't the mind, which as you point out is subvenient on the brain, not also be capable of doing the same thing? And then I guess that over time, constantly processing all the feedback from society, in order to stay in good social standing and physically survive, would cause our brains to develop certain hardwired tendencies, like collaborating, cooperating, and reciprocating."

"Interesting. You make a good argument. Any other points of view?"

In the back of the lecture hall, a young woman wearing a white "UCI Tennis" tee shirt raised her hand.

"Yes, Ms. Choi."

"I think there is another point of view to be offered here. I believe we are social beings not so much because our minds generate emergent properties from the neural workings of the brain, but because the human mind is a function of a larger, more complex but fully integrated system called the human being, which has spiritual as well as mental dimensions to it. Implicitly, the human mind knows it must form a social order, not only to cope with the dangers of its environment but also to allow for its spiritual expression. For example, how could we fully express all the dimensions of love that live in our souls without a social order—we need our families and friends, as partners in the process of spiritual journey. That is why we define civilization, as you have pointed out many times, in terms of the degree to which a group of individuals is willing to subjugate some measure of personal rights for the collective good of the group. I guess what I am arguing here is that we must look to a larger system of life, and perhaps a universal intelligence that is responsible for that larger self-organizing system, to comprehend the origin of our social nature as humans, in which case our brains simply help to execute what our minds already grasp."

Professor Kolowski seemed pleased with the different perspective. "Very intriguing argument, Ms. Choi. I like the more expansive focus of it. Thank you. For those of you who may not be familiar with the term, a 'self-organizing system' is one that always increases in complexity, continues to organize itself around a specific teleology, or goal, and is largely self-directed by some form of internal intelligence. "

Charlie noticed that he was suddenly feeling a little competitive. *Why wasn't my argument equally compelling?* He successfully fought the urge to raise his hand again and try to restate his position, and the Professor seemed interested in getting more of the class involved.

"Anyone else have an opinion?"

A very slight, and seemingly shy, young Korean girl raised her hand.

"Yes, Ms. Kim."

"Professor, I think both Charlie and Lucy make good points, but it seems to me that it all revolves around the dynamics of self-organizing systems. As you just mentioned, self-organizing systems are necessarily always becoming more complex. That means that once we humans branched out from our ancestors and began to acquire specialized skills, invent sophisticated languages, and develop more complex adaptive brains, our social systems started to self-organize into increasingly complex systems. Eventually, the only way for us to cope with this complexity was for our brains to become hardwired with some of the social instincts that are necessary to maintain complex social structures. In other words, if we did not learn to respond instinctively with as much altruism and compassion for others as we do in our instincts for self-preservation, we could not maintain the complex social structures and cultures we have today."

As impressed as Professor Kolowski had been with his first two students' suggestions, he was blown away by this third one. He tried not to show it, but he hesitated for a few seconds while he reveled in the realization that he was indeed a major catalyst in the formation of all these fertile minds. Finally, he came back to the issue at hand.

"I know we have a number of brilliant minds here at UCI, and I don't doubt that many are in this class, but I never cease to be amazed by all of you. That is not only a very powerful insight, Ms. Kim, but it is perhaps more brilliant than you realize. Yes, it is true, as Ms. Choi suggested, that there is something different about the human species and that it may involve some dimension we refer to as 'spiritual', but we are also incurably animals who have evolved over millions of years, in a self-organizing system of animal behavior that is governed by instinct, not thoughtful responses, which are, of course, unique to humans alone. As Ms. Kim has so articulately pointed out, our instincts may have become more sophisticated, but they are still instincts. There is evidence that chimps and bonobos, our closest primate cousins, have some altruistic instincts as well, but they are not as sophisticated and nuanced as ours. We are 'social beings' with brains that are hardwired for altruism, compassion, and reciprocal generosity, in large measure because we are social animals whose complex social systems demand that we possess certain instincts in order to maintain the equilibrium of our social structures. While it is true that we have developed very sophisticated cultures precisely to control some of the human instincts that might upset that equilibrium, I doubt that we could maintain the integrity of such cultures without the instincts for collaboration, reciprocity, and altruism having become hard-wired in our brains."

Charlie was furiously writing notes, both on what the professor had said and what he wanted to research later, just as the bell rang to end class.

chapter 10

CHARLIE EMERGED FROM the lecture hall into the bright mid-afternoon sun. Another perfect day—warm sun, cool air. Though hardly a bastion of architectural elegance, the UCI campus made Charlie feel at home. He loved the eucalyptus trees, but the scattered sections of pines and roving wisteria was what he enjoyed most. He always enjoyed his walk across campus on his way to the locker room.

As he came out of the locker room 20 minutes later, a few of his teammates were already on the field, taking early batting practice. Russ was in the box and spotted Charlie.

"Hey, Chas man, check it out. A little left handed BP, just like you suggested. What was the idea? I forget, but I have to say it's fun."

"Brain balance. Hitting from the side opposite your natural side makes the non-dominant side work harder, so you use both sets of hemispheric motor control areas and both the right and left visual cortices."

"Yeah, right. No wonder I couldn't remember. I sure hope that brain of yours never gets tagged by an inside fastball. Science might lose a Nobel Prize winner."

Charlie smiled. He secretly enjoyed being perceived as a bit of an egghead, at least as long as he continued to lead the team in batting average and no one questioned how good an athlete he was. He needed to feel accomplished in both domains to feel philosophically balanced, and as long as things were going well in the classroom and on the field, he was happy to take whatever ribbing his teammates wanted to dish out.

In truth, he craved the respect of his teammates, though he was not sure exactly why. Perhaps it was because his father had never had the chance to instill in his only son the confidence that he had what it took to make it in the world. Charlie remembered having read once that some child psychologists considered this the single most important thing a young male could acquire in his formative development years. Maybe he would always feel like he had to prove to himself that he did have what it takes. As he moved resolutely through his warm-up routine, Charlie kept his eyes focused on Russ and pondered what it was about him that made him so care free and wondered whether Russ carried that fundamental confidence that he could rise to the occasion when necessary.

Charlie nearly jumped out of his skin when Coach Cunningham came up behind him and grabbed him affectionately on both shoulder blades, squeezing firmly.

"Got my ace back today, right, Mr. Howell? The SC game is a distant memory by now, right?"

"Yessir, though technically, it's all in there some-where", Charlie deadpanned. It was his way of tweaking the Coach and letting him know, in case there was any question, how he liked to be mentored.

The Coach, himself a Masters graduate from Stan-ford, was more than happy to engage. "Enough with all your neuro babble, Howell. I need ball players with short memories. The last game is yesterday's news."

Charlie chuckled. "Don't worry, Coach. When it comes to baseball, I have a very short memory indeed. So who are we playing tomorrow?"

"Very funny, Howell. Come to think of it, we are just playing some no name weak sister, so perhaps I will just let you sit it out."

Charlie enjoyed the repartee, and the psychol-ogy—he knew that the Coach knew he would have to be on crutches to miss the UCLA game. "Let me double check my class schedule, and I will get back to you."

"Thanks, Howell. That's good to know." Coach suddenly jerked his head around. "Moyer, quit trying to become a switch hitter and get out of that cage. You know you can't hit a lick left-handed and you're wasting someone else's time in there."

Charlie was grateful that Russ wheeled and trot-ted out of the batter's box without explaining to the Coach that it was all Charlie's idea to try switch hitting. He grabbed his glove and headed for short. It always felt like going home, jogging out there to his position. No question, he loved being in the middle of the action. In fact, he liked being the center of attention too. May-be that was why he always wanted to be at bat when the game was on the line, no matter whether he had failed to deliver the night before or been hitless all day. The respect he earned when he came through seemed a powerful enough drug to last him until the next triumph, no matter the number of intervening failures.

chapter 11

SARAH SAT PERCHED on a fading yellow concrete bench, overlooking Balboa Peninsula and Newport Harbor, amusing herself. She loved coming down to the beach in the late afternoons, to meet the cool off shore breeze. She picked up her journal and started to record some of her reflections.

Had an interesting lunch with Charlie Howell the other day. That boy is nothing short of cute. And a mind to boot. Think I might accidently be strolling by Anteater Field tomorrow around 3.

I wonder why it is that when I feel attracted to a guy I always get this sense of chemistry. I wonder if it has to do with some spiritual connection. In fact, I wonder whether there is some connection between deep physical attraction for another person and the type of love God holds for each of us.

She stopped writing to watch a couple of kids running in and out of the water. She never had thought of herself as overly religious, but she knew that she had easy access to her spiritual self. The kids disappeared behind the ledge further down the beach, so Sarah picked up her pen.

Is there spirituality in the erotic? Now there's a question. I wonder where that came from. Really, though, why wouldn't that be true? Why can't the erotic be spiritual, and even the spiritual somewhat erotic? I want to have a spiritual connection with any guy I fall in love with, and certainly I want it to be equally physically pleasing, so what's wrong with thinking that the erotic and the spiritual are related? Note to self—think about this as a possible sub-theme in your great American novel, when you start to write it!

So, Charlie Howell. You made it to my journal, you lucky guy. First base, I would say. I doubt you would call it first base, but I understand how you guys think. Anyway, be careful over there at first, and don't get picked off!

Sarah laughed to herself, proud of her clever little baseball reference. Even if Charlie would never see it, she knew he would think it funny. She felt a deep sense of excitement settle into her body, and it caught her off guard. She wondered whether it might have registered on her face as well and looked around to see if anyone was watching. She closed her notebook and stared out at the ocean, letting the thoughts and feelings that emerged just ripple through her mind. After a few minutes, she retrieved the notebook and registered a last thought.

Sorry for the interruption there. I got a little distracted for a moment, and it's all your fault, Charlie Howell. Where was I? I guess my mind has shifted gears. Funny how that happens. I guess Charlie would say it was all due to some rush of chemicals into my brain when I got a little carried away back there with my thoughts. Or was it my emotions? Both I suppose. Hard to separate thought from emotion I bet. I should ask Charlie about that next time I see him. No doubt he will know the actual mechanics of what happens, but I guess I shouldn't tell him how it all came up!! Well, that's it for today.

chapter 12

SHUFFLING HIS FEET and kicking gently at the dirt around him, Charlie was suddenly aware of how distracted he felt. In the seventh inning of a tie game against UCLA, it was not exactly a good time for it, but there it was. He had spotted Sarah in the stands two innings ago as he approached the dugout between innings but had managed to block her out of his mind during his at bat, when he had doubled down the left field line to score a run and tie the game at 4. Now the thoughts would not go away.

Maybe this is more than a thought. Maybe it is connected to an emotion that I had not been aware of. Stop! We can't do this now. I am in the middle of a baseball game!

Charlie forced himself to focus intently on the catcher's right hand, as he flashed his four fingers and flicked them to his left. Change-up, inside. Turning his head quickly toward Doug Russell, his second baseman, Charlie made a big "O" with his mouth, waited a split second, until he was sure the batter's eyes were firmly fixed on the pitcher, and shifted subtly to his right. Still leaning, Charlie stared intently in at the batter, as the change-up moved down and in on his hands. The batter must have been looking for something inside, because he turned hard on the pitch, pulling his hands close to his body as swung, and lined the ball hard into the hole between short and third. Charlie felt a momentary surge of excitement, as he watched the play unfold in his mind, knowing he was going to snare the line drive, even before he left his feet. Now planed out, his whole body parallel to the ground, Charlie stretched with all his might and felt the ball smacking into his glove.

I knew it. I knew it. It was mine all the way. I love it when that happens.

Out number three. Charlie picked himself up, flipped the ball toward the mound before turning and tapping his glove against that of Jorge Maya, the third baseman, who had nonchalantly extended his glove toward Charlie in acknowledgement of his great play. Charlie liked that—the subtlety of it—the knowing tap on the butt or tap of the glove that exemplified voiceless acknowledgement athletes shared with each other, as if to say, "I know how great a play that was, but we have to be cool about it to really impress the fans." Of course, few fans really paid attention to that communication, thinking that their own wild screaming was the true testimony to a great play, but guys like Charlie always appreciated the small but genuine gesture from a teammate more than all the carrying on in the stands. Well, almost. In the stands *today* was one Sarah Wilson, and as he headed into the dugout, Charlie gave a quick glance to see if she were still there, hoping he would find out what *she* thought of the play.

She was gone. Disappointed, he ducked into the dugout and set his glove down, grabbed a helmet, and walked down to the bat rack. He was on deck.

Actually, Sarah was still in the stands, but she had moved. She had not wanted him to know she was there but was fairly certain he had spotted her a few innings ago. She was enjoying the game of being elusive but had not missed a thing on the field. *Wow, that was an awesome play. Guess that boy is pretty good. 'Course, I will never tell him.* She was aware though that part of her wanted to be able to search him out after the game, give him a big hug, and tell him how much she loved his diving stab in the seventh.

Charlie grabbed his bat, then walked out to the on deck circle. He had decided to use the old "lean on the bat" trick, so he could take a few more subtle glances around the stands for Sarah. Something told him she was still there. He kneeled down and wedged the bat against his opposite leg, pretending to stretch out his back, as he turned his head back and forth, subtly scanning. If she were right behind him, he would have no chance of seeing her. In front of him, Doug Pedroia had just drawn a walk, and Charlie refocused himself on the game.

As soon as Charlie came out on deck, Sarah ducked behind a large man in front of her, wearing a baby blue hat with "UCLA" scripted in gold across the front. Figuring Charlie would unconsciously divert his glances away from a big Bruin supporter, she felt safely hidden. It was all she could do to contain herself as she peeked around the large Bruin head, as Charlie drove the first pitch up the left center field alley for a stand-up double, driving in the go ahead run.

Charlie was hunkered down. Barely glancing into the UCI dugout to catch the jubilation, he stared straight ahead, as if boring lasers through the pitcher's head, in an effort to anticipate the location of the next pitch. But the thought came back anyway. It was just that way with the brain. You could concentrate your conscious mind as hard as you knew how and temporarily fix your consciousness on the object of your focus, but inevitably, those unconscious thoughts and emotions would always resurface.

I really never expected her to be here. I wonder why she came. And why can't I get her out of my mind. OK, OK, focus. We're playing baseball, for crying out loud.

Charlie looked over at the third base coach, in case there was a bunt sign on. Now up one in the seventh and no one out, Coach might try to get the "insurance run" over to third with one out. Nothing doing. His eyes locked in on the catcher, hoping to steal a sign. Nothing doing there either. In fact, the catcher and pitcher seemed so mixed up that the catcher called for time and strode out to the pitching mound. With time called, Charlie returned to the bag and consciously forced himself to stare toward the outfield. Immediately, his eyes fixed on the big red "W" of the Wienerschnitzel sign, and his mind wandered back to the previous year's game against the Bruins, when he had cleared that sign with a line drive, three run, walk off home run.

OK, it must be safe to turn around and peer into the stands again.

Charlie's eyes drifted over to the UCLA section of the stands. And there she was, half hidden behind some big lout in a blue cap. *The little devil. What is she up to? Was this some kind of teenager "I don't want you to know I like you" cat and mouse game going on?*

He sensed a fleeting disappointment. Then a spike of thrill. *She is here, after all, and she wouldn't be playing all these games unless she had some kind of good ulterior motive.*

The chase was on.

chapter 13

SARAH CAUGHT CHARLIE'S sudden glance and knew she had been made. *OK, now it's really time to leave. He probably thinks I am playing games with him because I am hot after him.* She figured she had to wait until Charlie's focus was back on the game, which would only take one or two pitches.

Now outside the stands she wondered what her little panic attack had been about. *What is so bad about Charlie knowing I came to the game and moved around a bit? For all he knew I just went to sit with some different friends. But why the quick exit? It's not like I have a ton of homework to do. Kate is off campus. Holly was working. Too late now. A girl has to maintain some dignity. Can't go back at this point.*

Sarah turned left out of the stadium and walked down the short hill to University Avenue. Across the divided four lane road was a cycling and jogging path that ran the full length of an environmentally protected area, which stretched from Michelson all the way down to the bay that fed into Newport Harbor. She decided to take a stroll and darted swiftly across the road at the first opportunity.

A couple of hundred yards down the path, she heard an enthusiastic cheer from the stadium and wondered if Charlie had made another spectacular play. It was time to forget him for a little while. She needed to be alone in her thoughts and actually found walking meditation the most useful way to do so.

C'mon, Sarah, how complicated could this be? Nick has been out of the picture for 6 months and you hardly even think about him any more. OK, the way it ended did hurt, but it shouldn't stop you from jumping right back up on the horse, should it? What is going on?

It was not an unusual conversation for her to be having with herself, but in fact she had a pretty good idea of what was going on. She was scared. Scared of actually picking a guy whom she could commit herself to completely. She hated to admit it to herself, but as much as her parents had affirmed her and encouraged her to be her own person, she never had been able to shake the fear that she would lose her sense of self if she committed herself to a man. It's why she kept picking jerks like Nick who not only didn't treat her that well but never had the real potential to become permanent fixtures in her life. It was a safe strategy.

She smiled to herself as she walked. She realized that she was becoming increasingly aware of what was behind her approach to dating and more honest with herself about what was really going on in her mind. Actually, it was beginning to feel good, that honesty. And maybe there were other good things yet to be experienced if she finally quit playing at relationship and tried to commit herself to one instead. Charlie Howell seemed like the kind of guy she could take a chance with, someone who had the patience and interest to talk her through some of her moments of panic. *Sarah Wilson, this guy is a catch. You should start paying a lot more attention to him.*

chapter 14

CHARLIE SHOWERED QUICKLY and headed out of the locker room. It had been a triumphant return to the field, following his earlier nightmare against USC, but he didn't feel like celebrating. Sarah Wilson was playing games with him, he was sure of that now, and it annoyed him. Besides he had homework to do. He spied Russ and Doug moving in his direction, so Charlie slipped quickly through the door and out into a typically beautiful southern California evening.

As he made his way back across campus to his apartment on Harvard Street, Charlie wondered why it was so difficult for him to celebrate his victories. After a game like that, in which he made two great plays in the field (*too bad Sarah didn't see that second one!*) and went 3 for 4, including the game winner, one might expect that he would have been begging the other guys to go have a celebratory beer or two, but instead all he could think of was that he had somewhat redeemed himself from the USC fiasco. And Sarah's disappearance after the game was bugging him too.

Peter A. Schuller

Ah, screw it. Not going to do me any good to worry about it. Might as well do something productive and read a few of my assignments for next week's Cognitive Behavior classes.

Charlie slid in the front door and grabbed a Diet Coke out of the refrigerator, before switching on his computer and opening up the articles he had downloaded earlier from Pub Med, dealing with the latest findings from a couple of Harvard professors on the neural correlates of consciousness. Soon he found himself completely engrossed. He could hardly believe how much their theory comported with his own notions of consciousness. He found one section particularly compelling.

"Consciousness should be viewed in many different contexts. First, each of us is born with a 'core consciousness' that contains and processes background emotions and provides a fundamental sense of self within a differentiated world. Core consciousness carries an ontological component. The nature of the core consciousness each of us brings into the world seems to carry certain distinct, genetically encoded characteristics that will help define our individual personalities and pathways in life. Although the brain is indeed plastic and therefore able to be reconfigured, and although we have some control over our minds and the thoughts we choose to generate, a fundamentally sad, quiet, withdrawn, and perhaps even depressed person is unlikely to transform herself into a into a happy-go-lucky, gregarious, joyful person. Nor will a creative artist ever think like an analytical accountant. For whatever

reason, just as we have distinct forms of intelligence and ways of thinking, each of us comes into this world with a core consciousness and perspective on life, which defines to some extent how we think, behave, and interact with our environments.

Core human consciousness unquestionably involves the experience of the "inner self" as an agent with causal power, and it starts with awareness. Because of all the different neurological and mental feedback systems in the human brain, we are aware that we exist in physical form and in relationship to other humans. We are aware when we are engaged in conscious thought, both of the thought itself and the process of thinking. We are able to identify an entity in our minds that is responsible for our actions, seeks meaning and purpose in life, and pursues answers to metaphysical questions.

This "genetically encoded" core consciousness is not static. While we may not undergo drastic changes in core consciousness during our lifetimes, we do experience shifts, which are engineered through the process of "gene expression". We are still learning about the mechanics of the human genome, but we do know that for the most part genes code for the production of proteins or turning on and off other genes. Humans are complex adaptive systems, and this type of "gene expression", involving the switching on and off of certain genes in response to changing conditions in the environment, is one of our most effective adaptive mechanisms. Gene expression of this kind can take place over long periods of time, engendering subtle changes in the brain and what emerges from it, or such gene expression can be swift and very specific, induced by various "epigenetic" processes. It seems likely that core human consciousness is highly influenced by the many forms and types of gene expression that occur throughout a human lifetime, as it encounters the many vagaries of its dynamic environment.

This form of consciousness is specifically contrasted to the phenomenal aspects of consciousness that dynamically define a person's moment to moment subjective life experiences. Whether engendered by the biochemical balance of neurotransmitters that happen to be coursing through our brains any given second or by the powerfully hard-wired network of synaptic connections that virtually guarantee in any given situation the brain's response to a certain set of stimuli, phenomenal consciousness essentially dictates the nature of our reality in a given instant. We are disposed to see, interpret, perceive, think, and act in each instance based on the state of extended consciousness that exists, quite mechanically, within our brains at a particular moment in time.

Victor Lamme has proposed the view that phenomenal consciousness depends on the level of feedforward and recurring processing that is taking place within the brain, and the area dealing with working memory in particular. (V. Lamme, 2004) Lamme's thesis is that essentially the nature of phenomenal consciousness one experiences is a function of how many and what type of different brain systems are linked together in a feedforward connection, as well as how much that connection of systems recurs in some form of closed loop processing. This theory suggests that at least to some extent, what we choose to focus our attention on at any given time can raise, if not altogether define, our consciousness about certain conditions, states, or phenomena.

Charlie stopped short and put down the article, as he suddenly thought about as the question he had asked himself after the USC game when he stood looking at strike three. Maybe it was a consciousness issue. Maybe the reason he had "known" that last pitch had been a strike even before the umpire called it was because his mind could process the incoming data at different levels, in parallel—both at a conscious level that was using just his visual perception processing system, tied to memories of thousands of other similar pictures, and also at an unconsciousness level, where feedforward processing was faster and could engage more systems than would ever be possible with the use of the conscious mind's "working memory". He wondered whether the same mental phenomena might be at work in connection to his thoughts and feelings about Sarah too. Did he "know" something more about her than his conscious mind was able to process? Suddenly, he was having some strange sensations about her. Something had entered his consciousness, but he had no idea what to make of it. There was simply no phenomenal consciousness of how he felt toward her that he could put his finger on. But at the same time, he knew there was something very special about her, and he also knew there was something he was going to have to do about it.

chapter 15

Sarah tossed in her bed, wrestling with the sheets. The pain was back, and more acute this time. Earlier in the afternoon, as she had been walking down toward the Back Bay, she had experienced a momentary stab of pain in her left leg but had thought very little of it. The body was always adjusting itself one way or another, so she thought it quite common to have the occasional little tweaks of pain or discomfort here and there, though she had never had that type of pain in her leg before. And it wasn't a cramp, but she had forgotten about it entirely by the time she had gone to bed. Then it was back, lingering this time, and more severe. She sat up and hoped it would subside shortly.

After two hours, Sarah quit trying to think about anything else. She couldn't focus on Charlie, the game that afternoon, or any of her feelings. There was only the pain now. It had climbed up her leg and gotten worse. It was time to do something. She tried to stand up but found she had little strength in her left side. A wave of panic ran through her as she reached for the phone and dialed 911. Moments after she was connected and gave her address to the dispatcher, she passed out.

chapter 16

NEWS TRAVELED FAST on the UCI campus. As Charlie headed across Campus Drive to his 11 o'clock Econ class, Russ caught up with him.

"You know Sarah Wilson don't you, Charlie?"

Charlie's mind immediately staring racing. *Jeez, what did Russ know? How would anybody know what I feel for Sarah? I haven't said anything, have I?*

He looked at Russ again and noticed the seriousness on his face. Charlie was confused. *If I am not about to be ribbed about Sarah, what is going on?* He nodded back at Russ, "Yeah, of course, why, what's up?"

"She's in critical condition at Saddleback. Something about her heart."

Charlie's knees practically gave way. "What?! You're kidding. No way. How?"

Russ noticed. "Charlie, you OK? Is there something I don't know about between you and Sarah?"

"Ah, no, no. Well, I mean I don't know. It just kind of started the other day, but…"

"Oh, man, I had no idea. I'm sorry. If I had known, I wouldn't have just blurted it out like that."

"Russ, like I told you, you couldn't have known. I don't really know. Sorry, I am a little confused right now. But I can tell you I don't much feel like going to Econ right now. Can I borrow your car? I think I need to go down to the hospital and find out what I can."

Russ saw the look in Charlie's eye and immediately changed into the role of concerned teammate. "I'll drive you down. Wanted to skip my Spanish class anyway."

"Thanks, Russ. You're a good man."

chapter 17

WHEN HE WAS upset, it was easier for Charlie to talk than to sit quietly. Somehow the mere process of talking released some of the emotion and feelings of stress generated in his brain. During a particularly boring practice early last week, Charlie had thought more about that whole phenomenon.

Maybe it's related to the concept of "working memory" we have been discussing in class, he thought. *If my working memory is forced to pull together the different brain systems for language, speech, and object association in order to help me articulate my thoughts and feelings, maybe in the process some of the energy that would otherwise be devoted to churning up more emotion gets short circuited. Or maybe it is just the other way around— the more I talk, the more my motor systems tap into the systems that process emotions, thereby releasing and dissipating them.*

Now he just wanted to talk with Russ, as they crept along the 405 in heavy traffic, in the direction of Saddleback Hospital. Theory or no theory, it felt good to just get it out of him, and there was no doubt that some strong emotions, or feelings—he wasn't sure which—had been churned up in his mind over the last 30 minutes.

"You know, Russ, I had lunch with her yesterday, then she came to the game. I mean, we have been friends for awhile, and occasionally I would run into her, have lunch, and just talk. But yesterday was different."

"How so?"

"Honestly, I don't think I could tell you exactly, but something was different. Our lunch conversation seemed more intimate. And then she just showed up at the game. Never mentioned she was thinking about coming or where she might be sitting. I just happened to see her once when I was scanning the stands between innings."

"Well it didn't seem to affect your performance too badly!"

"I can tell you I was a little distracted once or twice. Glad you couldn't tell."

"And how do you feel about it—about her I mean?"

"Not sure I know that either, Russ. It's all kind of coming at me fast. But when you told me about her, it sure hit me hard, so I must already have some feelings I haven't yet figured out."

"Yeah, well, hopefully this traffic won't get any worse and we can get over to the hospital soon to find out."

Charlie hesitated, then decided to plunge ahead. He didn't really know Russ that well but needed to talk, to anyone.

"Hey, Russ, what's your experience with women?"

"Not too bad, but is that the right subject for this moment?"

"No, Russ, I don't mean that way. I mean, what do you know about love and women?"

"Probably not too much. Why?"

"Neither do I. I just thought it would help me to sort out what is going through my mind right now. I understand that neuroscience treats feelings and thoughts quite similarly—meaning they both draw on cognitive processes."

"Yeah, well, if you start talking like that again, Charlie, you will pretty much convince me that you don't know anything about love. Do you ever give your mind a break?"

"Admittedly not too often. But c'mon, Russ, who says that love only comes from the heart? Only poets, and that's because they don't know science. I say science can help us know the mind, the heart—whatever that is—and the experiences of love better than philosophy or psychology, or even English Lit! In fact, I bet what most people think of as the "heart" is primarily a function of mind, located in the brain, not the chest."

"Radical thinking, my dear boy. There are a lot of Eastern philosophers who would not agree with you. I believe that they would say the heart exists within the whole of the body. And I may not know much about love, but I recommend you don't take that approach in matters of romance!"

"OK, OK, it's the blind leading the blind here, but seriously, science can prove that emotions are chemically signaled, and therefore effectively processed in the brain, and some noted neuroscientists like Damasio and LeDoux have done a number of experiments suggesting that the brain also cognitively develops certain feelings as ways of both managing and embellishing emotions, so why couldn't the experience of love be precisely that—deep-seated emotions that have been contextually transformed into feelings of the heart?"

"But guys like Deepak Chopra are equally convinced that the biochemistry of emotion is processed throughout the entire neurological system, not just the part contained in the brain."

Charlie turned abruptly in his seat and gave Russ a long, intentionally respectful stare. "Why, Russ, you philosopher you! I had no idea."

"Always like to keep 'em guessing a little, Charlie. Always keep them guessing."

The conversation had worked to lighten Charlie's mood somewhat. The traffic had finally broken free, as Russ maneuvered his red Miata into the right hand land so they could catch the exit at El Toro and proceed onto Valencia. Two minutes later, Russ turned into the parking lot.

chapter 18

RUSS THOUGHT CHARLIE must have reached the top steps of the hospital faster than he normally got down the line from home to first, which was saying a lot. At the Information Desk, Charlie politely asked if Sarah Wilson had been admitted.

"Are you a relative?" the lady behind the desk inquired.

"Well, no, just a friend."

She checked her computer.

"Well, then, I can tell you that there is a Sarah Wilson who has been admitted, but I am afraid that is all I can tell you."

Charlie blanched. "Why is that?"

"HIPPA regulations."

"What?"

"HIPPA. The federal guidelines regarding medical patient privacy. We cannot share a patient's information with just anybody."

"And I am not just anybody. I am a friend, a good friend."

"Sorry, sir, HIPPA doesn't make those distinctions."

"Well, I already know that she is in intensive care. Can you tell me whether she is still there?"

"No, sorry."

"Who is her doctor? Can you at least tell me that?"

"Yes, that is quite all right. It's Dr. Galloway. But he is most likely in surgery right now."

"Great. How do I get any information?!"

"Do you know her parents? I am sure they must have been contacted by now."

"No, I don't. Sarah and I are at UCI together. I don't even know where her parents live."

"I am terribly sorry. You seem like a nice fellow, but as they say, my hands are tied."

"Yes, I can see that they are. Guess we came down here for nothing Russ. Might as well head back and grab lunch before baseball practice."

"You boys play for UCI?"

Charlie's hopes jumped a notch. "Why, yes, we do, ma'am. Russ here is our catcher. I play shortstop."

"Oh, I love baseball, and you boys are doing pretty well this year, I see."

"Holding our own against the big boys, that's about all you can ask for."

Russ was impressed. He didn't know Charlie had a 'pour on the charm' side, but he was doing pretty well.

"Well, you just keep at it. I'm rooting for you."

Charlie realized there wasn't going to be any change of the lady's mind after all, even if they were charming baseball players from UCI. His mother had always taught him to be a gentleman in defeat though, so he thanked the lady and headed for the exit. Russ shook his head and smiled. That was exactly why Russ wanted Charlie Howell as his captain—always a class act.

chapter 19

CHARLIE TOOK HIS requisite batting practice hacks, lining ball after ball sharply to right and left field, though clearly displaying uncharacteristic indifference. Coach Cunningham was the first to notice.

"You OK, Charlie? I know you had a great game yesterday, but it's not like you to think you don't need to practice hard every day."

"No, nothing like that, Coach. Just a lot on my mind."

"Yeah, fine. No problem. Take some infield, and let me know if it's anything you want to talk about."

"A friend of mine. She's in critical condition down at Saddleback, but Russ and I couldn't find out anything more when we went down this morning."

"Goodness. Sorry to hear that. A student here?"

"Yeah, Sarah Wilson."

"She a *close* friend, Charlie? You know that stuff is none of my business and that I am good about staying out your personal lives, but if you want to talk about it, we can do that."

"Yeah, no sweat, Coach. I appreciate that. Yes, she is a special friend, but we aren't dating or anything. It's different. Still, maybe I was closer than I thought. I am pretty upset."

"Do what you need to, Charlie. If it helps to be distracted by practice, we'll take some infield. If not, why don't you call it a day?"

"Thanks, Coach. I think I will stick it out."

When he got out to short and starting taking some ground balls, he was still just going through the motions. His mind wouldn't let go of an image—one of Sarah, possibly hooked up to oxygen and all sorts of heart monitors, unconscious and a world away. He remembered what he had read in the article on consciousness the night before—it seemed that he kept linking his memories of Sarah and their conversations with projections out of his brain's visual imaging system then running them over and over again in some type of closed feedback loop. *Is this why I just can't get the image out of my mind? Is that effectively what phenomenal consciousness is?* He thought about the countless times that his mind had been stuck in a rut—thinking endlessly about an at bat he wished he could have back, or something he said to a friend he wished he hadn't—all those times when his mind was virtually consumed by a single thought, or feeling. *So, let's see, if consciousness really is simply a matter of the brain's working in a certain way, perhaps I could consciously will my brain to alter its activities, which would have to shift my consciousness.*

A ball scooted up the middle, within the range where, during a game, Charlie would instinctively have made a move on it, but this was practice and his mind was otherwise occupied. He let it bounce into center field. A surge of excitement raced through him. Then he noticed that thoughts of Sarah had temporarily disappeared while he was deep in thought about this notion of consciousness.

Lamme was right—when your brain shifts to different feedforward processing of new stimuli, especially if it requires the deployment of different brain functions, your consciousness shifts. Or once you take your attention off something, like I did with that ground ball, my consciousness moves.

Charlie suddenly found himself totally absorbed, not in baseball and ground balls but in the many instances where he remembered his consciousness had been consumed by a single thought or emotion and how hard it often was to escape from such states. It struck him that indeed the brain must rely heavily on feedforward systems which send information about goals, needs, and strategies into different parts of the brain, as well as the feedback systems that report back on progress related to those goals, needs, and strategies. *So all you have to do is change the 'initial conditions', as they say in theoretical science! All I have to do is refocus my attention on something else, whether it involves external stimuli or internal thoughts, and I can start a new set of feedforward and feedback systems, a whole new experience of phenomenal consciousness. How cool.*

Charlie figured that it would certainly make sense that consciousness would essentially emerge from the cumulative effect of such feedforward and feedback systems, and he could well understand how once one set of those systems became firmly locked in, it might be difficult to escape its influences. *So maybe that's what happens when I am in the "zone" and can focus so intently on a given pitch, thinking about nothing else, or when I feel this overwhelming sense of attraction to Sarah, virtually consuming my consciousness—it must be that just one set of feedforward and feedback systems is domi-nating my working memory and thought processes!!*

Without even thinking about what his teammates might be wondering, Charlie trotted off the field, to-ward the dugout. He needed to focus. This could be a major breakthrough, not only in the practical ways it could help him perform on the diamond, but in terms of his studies, perhaps even his life's work to come. Back behind the plate, Russ looked over at Charlie as he sat down in the dugout and wondered what was going on.

chapter 20

CHARLIE BORROWED RUSS' car for the next three days and drove the 8 miles to Saddleback Hospital, hoping to either run into Sarah's parents or get some news on her. Finally, just as he was about to leave, he heard a women's voice say,

"Yes, I am Mrs. Wilson. What is it?"

"There is a call for you, ma'am. Dr. Galloway."

"Oh, thank you. Where can I take it?"

"Right over there at that phone."

Charlie shuffled closer and leaned in, not wanting to be noticed.

"Yes, thank you, doctor. That's great. I will be right up."

She turned toward the elevators and Charlie followed quickly, catching up in only five strides.

"Excuse me, Mrs. Wilson?"

She turned, somewhat startled. "Yes, do I know you?"

"No, I am sorry, ma'am. My name is Charlie Howell. I am a friend of Sarah's and have been coming down here for the last four days trying to find out how she is doing, but they won't tell me. I was just about to leave when I heard them call your name. I am sorry to intrude, but could you at least tell me how she is doing."

"Yes, of course. I mean I need to go find out myself. They have just moved her out of ICU. Charlie, is it? Listen, dear, let me go see her, and I will come back shortly. Can you wait?"

It was definitely not his first choice, but he could live with it. At least the end of this lousy waiting game was in sight. "Sure, thank you so much, Mrs. Wilson."

"Call me Ann. I will be back when I can."

Forty minutes later, Ann Wilson returned. Charlie had a hard time reading her expression.

"She is conscious and improving, Charlie. Actually, when I mentioned you were downstairs, she seemed to perk up even more. It's none of my business, of course, Charlie, but a mother knows certain things, and…" She seemed to catch herself on a thought, almost as though some preset circuit breaker in her brain had been tripped, before she continued. "Well, we don't need to go down that path right now. As to her condition, I admit I am still in a bit of a shock. Thank goodness my husband and I were home when someone from the university called. We had just returned from a long weekend in Bermuda. Apparently, she has contracted some type of virus that has invaded her heart. The doctor would not give me much more, and to be honest I am not sure how much more he even knows himself. They can be very cautious these days, those doctors."

She stopped, seeming to catch her breath, but then it appeared she did not know what else to say. She apparently had initially felt quite comfortable relaying the medical information to Charlie, then seemed to remember he was a virtual stranger. Charlie felt a little awkward too.

"Thank you, Mrs. Wilson, I mean Ann. I am sure this is quite difficult for you, and I appreciate your sharing what you know with me. Hopefully, we will all know more in the next couple of days. Will you be staying awhile?"

"Frank—my husband—will have to go back in a few days. I will stay indefinitely. Of course, I have no idea what the recovery process is for something like this."

"Well, if there is anything I can do, please let me know. I don't own a car, but I can borrow a friend's if you need a ride any place."

"Thanks, Charlie, but we have already hired a car. Fortunately, I have a cousin who lives in Lake Forest, so I can stay there and be quite close. I imagine when Sarah feels up to visitors, I will see you here again. I am sure she would like to see you."

Charlie thought she added that last part for a purpose but decided to let sleeping dogs lie. "Right, well, I better be getting back to school. Thank you so much again. Please tell Sarah I am thinking of her and will give her a call tomorrow to see how she is."

"I will be happy to, Charlie. It was a pleasure meeting you."

chapter 21

By the following week, Sarah was feeling better, though according to the doctor she was still not out of the woods. Viruses are nasty and somewhat unpredictable, he told Sarah and her mother. You had to be careful and vigilant, see how the body responded.

When Sarah finally did feel up to having Charlie as a visitor, her mood was still somewhat somber, but clearly she had spent some time with her mother sprucing up a bit.

He surprised her, and himself, when he handed her the flowers he had bought, then leaned over and gave her a peck on the cheek.

"How are you feeling, Sarah?"

"I am doing better, thank you Charlie. It's good to see you. Mom says you have been hanging around downstairs like an expectant father."

Charlie flushed with embarrassment, which thankfully Ann Wilson took as her cue to leave the two of them alone, and she announced she was going down the hall for a cup of coffee.

"I was worried, of course. I couldn't believe it really. You know, we had just had a great lunch the day before and you were fine then. I was concerned, maybe even a bit scared I guess, because I had no idea what it was, until your mom told me, but that was at least three days or four days after you got here."

"Yeah, I know. I guess I didn't have time to get scared, it happened so fast. I just woke up here and found my parents at my bedside. Obviously, when the doctor explained what had happened and what is still going on, I got a bit spooked, but I am doing pretty well now in that department. I am a very spiritual person, Charlie, so that helps."

"Glad to hear that. Maybe you can share more of that—I mean your experience and thinking about that aspect of life—with me sometime."

"I would like that, Charlie. I really would."

"Well, I guess I better not stay long. I am sure you are supposed to get a lot of rest for that heart of yours."

"Yes, but you have done it some good by coming to see me, Charlie. And I was very touched when Mom told me you had been coming down here every day to see how I was doing. Sorry about how all that government red tape made it so difficult."

"Thanks, but don't worry about that. I couldn't just sit around at the dorm or in the library anyway—my mind would have been here, so my body might as well have been too."

"You're a good man, Charlie Brown. And a good friend too. Hey, maybe that's what I will call you, Charlie Brown."

Charlie smiled, sort of. "Don't you dare."

Ann Wilson had returned, apparently ever mindful of the time and concerned that her daughter might get fatigued by too long a visit, especially from this fellow who seemed to be more than just a friend. Charlie decided to pass on the goodbye kiss and sidled toward the door.

"Take care, Sarah. I will be back soon. Nice to see you again, Ann."

Sarah sat up slightly. "I'm holding you to that promise, Charlie Brown."

Ann looked confused. "Charlie Brown?

Sarah rolled her eyes. "Mom, it's just a tease. And trust me no one is less like Charlie Brown that that guy!"

"I see. So exactly who is this guy? More than a friend I am guessing."

Sarah demurred. She was getting tired and didn't have the energy to go down that road. "Well, Mum, he might just be the next Red Sox shortstop in a few years."

Ann Wilson adored the Red Sox. "Really?"

"Really. Now, I am feeling a bit sleepy, so could you lower my bed back down a little for me?"

"Sure, Sweetie. The Red Sox, huh?"

Sarah grinned to herself. It was so easy to get her mom going.

chapter 22

CHARLIE COULD HARDLY wait for the game to end. Cal State Fullerton was always a formidable foe, and supposedly the Red Sox had sent another scout to have a look at him, but Charlie had other things on his mind. Sarah's condition had been improving over the last several days and earlier in the day, she had texted him on his cell phone, asking him to come visit her. Fortunately, Charlie had the kind of talent that allowed him to perform well, even when he was distracted. He called it his Auto Pilot game. Of course, he figured that, like any good airline captain, one had to choose the appropriate times to turn on the Auto Pilot. The final out happened when the Cal State catcher pounded a ground ball up the middle, which Charlie knocked down with a diving stab, then calmly gathered up and fired to first, beating the slow footed runner by two steps, preserving a 5-3 victory.

Charlie dressed quickly and stepped over to Russ' locker.

"Hey, man, can I borrow your car again?"

"Sure, going to see Sarah?"

"Yeah."

"What about the scout, don't you need to talk to him or anything?"

"Don't think so, Russ. He saw what he came for, one way or the other, I am sure."

"Yeah, but don't they like to talk to you at all, find out what you are like personally, or how you think? They have to be impressed with guys like you. Don't you at least have the urge to impress them with your neurospeak?"

"No, oddly enough they haven't said anything to me about any of that. I agree, I would have thought that was important, as much money as they pay to find out if you are any good. In fact, I am always amazed when I read that some superstar has some major psychological issue. You would have thought they had scouted all that stuff out by then. But they will have to come find me. I am not about to seem like I am promoting myself."

"Why not? It's not like it could really hurt, or that you don't have a vested interest in promoting Charlie Howell's going high in the draft."

Charlie found he actually did not have a good answer to that question, either for Russ or himself. He thought perhaps when he had a chance he would examine that issue a little more. *Why exactly am I so averse to promoting myself? Does that somehow make me feel like I am not good enough to be selected, that they will only draft me because I pushed so hard?* He shifted his attention back to Russ. "I don't know, Russ. Just doesn't seem like it would really matter. I mean, if they want to know something that's important to them, they will ask, right?"

Russ shook his head for a good ten seconds before looking up. "You know, Charlie, for a really smart guy, you can sure be naïve. You don't need a whole lot of help from me, but take my advice on this one— never assume some organization knows what it really wants, or even what is good for it. I learned that from my father, who has been a management consultant for the last ten years and who used to come home practically ever day regaling my mom and me with stories of how clueless some of his clients were about what they were up to."

Charlie suddenly forgot about Sarah and began to listen intently. "Clueless?"

"Yeah, Charlie, clueless. And I doubt that baseball operations are much better at their games than banks or car companies are at theirs. Hell, you might even shock them out of their skyboxes if you sat down and talked with them about one of your countless ideas about the mind."

"These are scouts we're talking about here, Russ. I might also scare them away."

"Good point. I heard that when Billy Beane started his whole new approach to the game at Oakland, he eventually had to sack all the old scouts because they just didn't believe in statistics. All they wanted to know was how fast a guy could pitch, how fast he could get down the line, or how far he could hit a baseball." Russ started laughing. "Ironically, all the scouts had Billy Beane himself pegged as a phenom, but as it turned out he was a head case who couldn't deal with the pressure at the major league level. I think it took the additional irony of Beane's quitting baseball and going into baseball *management* to even wake the major league organizations up to the idea that they might want to consider a prospect's mental capabilities, let alone evaluate him as both a physical and mental being."

"Interesting, Russ. My cousin read *Moneyball* and told me a little about it, but I had not heard that about Billy Beane."

"Ya see, Charlie, occasionally you have to put those neuroscience tomes aside and get yourself some practical learning. And go catch that scout before you go to the hospital", Russ ordered, tossing him the car keys.

chapter 23

As IT TURNED out, Charlie didn't have to go looking for Bob Neal, the chief scout for the Boston Red Sox. When Charlie emerged from the locker room, Neal was waiting for him. The bigger surprise for Charlie, however, came after Neal had introduced himself, when he explained that he had briefly spent time in the minors but had decided to pursue a doctorate in psychology. *I guess Russ was right,* Charlie thought to himself. *Whether it was Billy Beane or something else, scouts sure have changed.*

"It's a pleasure meeting you, Dr. Neal. I appreciate your coming out here to see me. I trust you had other business in the area as well."

"No, actually, Charlie, I came just to see you. And please call me Bob! I am on a tight schedule, though. Can you have dinner with me tonight?"

Charlie hesitated. He had his mind set on seeing Sarah and tried to quickly calculate if he had time to see her, have dinner with Neal, and get to his homework. Well, his homework could wait, but it would certainly cut into his time with Sarah.

"Could we do it later, around 8:30?"

"Sure, Charlie. I have no problem with that. Where would you like to go and do you have a car?"

"Yeah. I can meet you at Houston's. It's in Park Place shopping center, at the corner of Jamboree and Michelson. Where are you staying?"

"I am at the Hyatt, on Main. I know where Jamboree is from there. Where is Michelson?"

"First light across the highway from where you will be. Go north on Main, turn left on Jamboree, and you will actually see the Houstons on your left right after you cross over the 405. Go left on Michelson and left again into Park Place."

"Sounds easy enough, even for a PhD."

Neal smiled warmly, but Charlie thought there might have been a subtle message buried in his quip. And if that were true, they were going to enjoy each other's company.

"Good, see you at 8:30 then. If you have any trouble, my cell number is 949 887 2356."

"Thanks. Mine is 617 354 4520. And by the way, Charlie, having seen you in action, I understand why the organization is so high on you. Until later, then."

Charlie knew there was a message folded into Neal's parting comment, and it wasn't that subtle either. He could think about it a little longer on his way back from the hospital, though. Sarah was waiting.

chapter 24

SARAH WILSON NOT only didn't look like she was sick, she looked like she could work a runway that evening. Apparently, since Charlie had last seen her, she had been allowed to dress and spend some time sitting in a chair, even take an occasional brief stroll around the ward. When Charlie arrived, she left her chair to greet him, her light blue chiffon blouse falling gracefully over her stylish jeans, barely covering her firm belly. Charlie suspected that Sarah might have put considerable thought into what wardrobe choice would make the best statement, while still passing muster with her mom.

As they approached, Charlie leaned forward and gave her a warm hug.

"Sarah, you look great. How do you feel?"

Sarah hesitated a moment, apparently processing the compliment and taking time to congratulate herself, and Kate, on their selections.

"Thank you, Charlie, and actually, I do feel quite well. They said they might let me go early next week, depending on what the tests show. They think there might be some damage to my heart and they are trying to get a better read, as the muscle begins to heal. And how are you doing? My scouts tell me you had a pretty good game today."

Charlie was in a playful mood. "Really? You have scouts? Isn't that expensive?"

Sarah smiled. "Not really. Sometimes I use bribes, sometimes blackmail. It all works out pretty well."

"Might I know who they are? I mean, Russ just advised me that I should start paying better attention to the Big League scouts when they show up, so maybe the same is true for your scouts."

"Really? Big League Scouts? Who?"

"Don't you try to change the subject that fast. But yeah, there have been a few lately, and in fact I am having dinner tonight with one from the Red Sox."

Sarah feigned hurt. "You got a better offer this evening?"

"Most reluctantly, of course, but I thought it would be rude, what with his coming all the way out here from Boston to see me."

"I am just kidding. I think it's fantastic, congratulations. She moved closer, then quickly snatched a kiss, retreating to a distance that indicated the gesture was "just as a friend, of course."

"Thanks. I will let you know how it goes. So who's your spy—I mean 'scout'?"

"Very funny. Hey, what's wrong with a girl wanting to know what's going on out there in the world while she's stuck in a silly hospital?"

"Fair enough. Well, if you are not going to divulge sources, how about at least telling me what was in the report?"

"Fishing for a compliment now, huh?"

"Such cynicism, Sarah. It doesn't become you."

Charlie saw that Sarah's complexion had changed. Her mouth curled up on one side and moisture quickly appeared in her eyes. When she caught him looking at her, she put out her hand and touched his.

"I'm sorry, Charlie. It's been a long day, in fact a long week. I just really wanted to see you. I didn't mean to…."

"Oh, no, it's my fault. I'm sorry. I really didn't mean it seriously. In fact, you are the complete antithesis of a cynic. It's one of the things that's so charming about you."

Sarah smiled, but the tears came anyway, perhaps started by a process that had begun before Charlie started to speak, perhaps brought on by the realization of how much she cared for him and just wanted to be held, to be comforted in a way that would wash away the last ten days of sitting around worrying about her condition.

Instinctively, Charlie clutched her hand, pulled her gently to him and held her in his arms.

After a few minutes, Sarah finally spoke. "Thank you, I needed that. Can we just sit awhile and talk for a bit?"

chapter 25

IT TOOK SARAH some time before she wanted to say anything to him. It felt so good just to be near him, to feel his presence, which she experienced as both physically powerful and emotionally comforting. Charlie thought it would be better to simply wait for her to initiate whatever she wanted and patiently tried to focus on what might be going through her mind. Whatever he imagined it might be, though, he was pretty sure he would be wrong. *Thinking you could read another's person's mind is elusive at best, dangerous at worst,* he reminded himself. Sarah began to sit more upright in her chair.

"Charlie, remember the other day when you asked if we could talk more about spiritual matters some time?"

"Yeah."

"Could we do that now?"

"Sure. Anything in particular? I told you I am a novice in that domain, right?"

"That's what you said, yes, but I am not looking for experts. I just want to talk, with you."

Peter A. Schuller

"Has the last ten days been difficult for you, spiritually, I mean?"

"No, not at all. In fact, my spirituality has helped see me through some of my fears and worry. I have always had a deep sense of myself—I guess that's the best way to describe it—something that made me know about a Creator who took care in forming me and a purposefulness to my life to go along with it. I have no idea what that purpose is, whether it revolves around a career, a family, a role, or just a way of being perhaps, but I know there is some underlying meaning to who I am and what I am doing here in this life."

"Meaning, I guess, that you believe there is more than just this life."

"Oh, yes. I am not a hundred percent clear on what I think about that either, mind you. But I know there is a meaning to my life and that what I do in some way affects how the entire universe proceeds. It's what some Christians call co-creationism, the idea that we are agents of God's creativity and help define by our thoughts and actions the world we live in. Other religions and spiritual practices have similar notions, I think."

"That sounds pretty lofty. I would just be happy if I got to spend a year playing major league baseball, had a healthy family, and learned a thing or two about the way our minds work—and maybe wrote a book or two about it. But I don't think anyone would care 100 years from now what old Charlie Howell had done."

"Well, Charlie. I do think they would care, but that's not exactly what I meant. I am not concerned about my "legacy" as a person, but the contribution I make to the spiritual evolution of all humanity. It's more of a 'quantum' thing, I suppose, the notion that whatever choices we make have some effect at a quantum level of reality and that somehow what happens in the quantum world manifests in physical reality too. I think God must have some form of Intelligence that must at some level have given impetus to this universe of ours, and ultimately all the forces of nature, evolution, and what not. We have some of that same Intelligence in us too, and I think humans were always intended to be carriers of the divine spark, to work within all the dynamics and constraints of our universe but nevertheless have an effect on how it turns out. That is why one of my favorite myths is about how Prometheus stole fire from the gods and brought it to humanity."

"Awesome, Sarah. I had no idea you were that mindful about such things."

"Oh, yes, Charlie. I do consider myself mostly spiritually inclined, because I have met many religious people who don't seem to have any awareness of their divine nature and the responsibility that goes along with it. I am an Episcopalian by upbringing, and I very much like Episcopal theology, but I tend to integrate other religious practices into my belief system as well, especially Buddhism. I think the Buddhists are wonderful in their attitudes toward certain aspects of life, like detachment, expectations, and suffering. Eastern religions and philosophies tend to be based on both thoughtful underpinnings and disciplined practice. Western religions, on the other hand, have sought to dominate philosophy and therefore emphasize liturgy and doctrine. Unfortunately, in many cases those doctrines have been used, quite heavy handedly, to 'indoctrinate', very much distorting the true messages of Christ, which, ironically, so many of them claim as their savior or prophet."

Charlie tried his John Wayne imitation. "Whoa, slow down little lady."

"Sorry. I do get charged up about this stuff."

"Let's go back to Episcopal theology. What do you like about it and why?"

"It's a theology that encourages you to think and to search for your own belief system. It's very spiritual really, because while it does promote the use of reason, Episcopal theology expects you to open up your *entire* mind—including body and soul—to the nature of God and Creation. It adopts the approach that our minds are reflective of divine nature and perfect instruments to help us understand who God is and what we are doing here. And Episcopal theology is flexible enough to accommodate a broad range of personal expressions of faith and prayer life. For example, Taize prayer, which is from France, is a very old and spiritually based ritual. But mostly I like the Episcopal theology because it presupposes that you will always be searching for God and struggling with your beliefs, as you evolve in your spiritual understanding and growth, as you learn that the purpose of life is to serve others. It's very process oriented—God and the purpose of life are always to some extent mysteries to be pursued."

Charlie suddenly found himself in a place he had never been before. His mind seemed relaxed, and he was enjoying just sitting and listening. Not the same way he would engross himself in an intriguing lecture, completely focused on the subject matter and making sure he was absorbing everything. This was different. Sarah's words were speaking to another part of him. And he found it intriguing that a religious practice could be cerebral, even process oriented.

"That does sound like a comforting and enabling belief system, Sarah."

"Oh, it's more than that, Charlie. Sometimes when I am in church, I get this ecstatic feeling that comes over me, takes hold of my whole body, and bathes it in warmth that can hardly be described. For some reason, I have always supposed that making love to someone with whom you shared true emotional intimacy would be sort of like that too—an indescribable merger of the heart and soul."

Charlie shifted nervously in his chair. In part because he was not really comfortable talking about making love, especially with a woman, and in part because he found himself immediately wondering what it would be like to have sex with Sarah. She noticed his uneasiness.

"Well, I guess we shouldn't go down that road right now. Let's stick to spirituality and religion. What about you, Charlie? What are your beliefs? Actually, I think you referred to a belief 'system', right?"

"Yes, that's true. As you know, I am fascinated by the mind and the workings of the brain that create the mind, and it is true, I love systems of all sorts. Because the brain is essentially one large, integrated system of

125

sub-systems that perform all manner of autonomous and cognitive functions, I suspect that we all develop *systems* of beliefs, based on who are parents are and what they believe, what cultures we were brought up in, how we think, what type of consciousness we carry around in our minds, and dozens of other similar factors."

"I see. And where does faith fit into that formula?"

Charlie noticed Sarah's particular tone when she said the word "formula". It sounded a little edgy to him, but he decided to ignore it.

"Oh, I would say faith beliefs fit quite easily into my construct. A large part of who we are relates to the core consciousness we bring into this world with us, and I believe that consciousness is somehow embedded in the neurology of our brains, from birth. Of course, we have countless experiences in life that offer us opportunities to examine and even change different aspects of our consciousness—I am an existentialist to be sure—but it seems to me that so much of what goes on in our belief systems relates to the way our brains work. You know, even the belief systems of your ancestors, and other aspects of your cultural history, are somehow embedded in the neurodynamics of your brain. By neurodyanmics, I mean not just the unique neurological engineering and characteristics of your brain but the many "emergent properties" that are produced by the complex interconnection of innumerable systems within it. I have no doubt that what you believe, for example, is a product in some measure of not only what you have cognitively worked out for yourself in the last several years but what you have surmised from the non-cognitive experiences you had as a child, especially those special moments in church you talked about."

"I am glad you included that last bit, Charlie, because I think my beliefs are much more spiritually engendered than cognitively derived."

"But what do you mean by 'spiritually engendered'? What is the process by which that would take place? I mean, in the brain, of course. Or possibly the mind. I am sure that what we call the mind, for want of a better term, involves more than just the output and activities of the brain. After all the human body has a very sophisticated neurological system, of which the brain is only a part. I expect our minds 'emerge' from the combination of many different activities within our bodies."

Sarah looked somewhat relieved. "Well, I think we agree on that. To be honest, I haven't studied much about the brain, so I would not really be in a good position to speculate, but I am sure that we are divine in some part of our nature, I am sure that we can receive and transmit energetic impulses that have "information" embedded in them, and I therefore believe that in some manner our bodies are able to energetically connect to the divine Spirit of the Creator that created us and cares for us. I call that a spiritual connection, and so for me my awareness of and participation in that connection is what I think of as my spirituality."

Charlie smiled deep within himself. He could not remember having had a more enriching conversation. Not only was this different perspective opening up new vistas in his mind, but it was coming from a perfectly articulate, engaging, beautiful young woman, to whom he was becoming more and more physically attracted by the minute. Just then some distant alarm went off in his head. *Dinner with Neal.* Damn. Just as it was getting good, he would have to go.

"Sarah, I hate to do this, but I have to cut this short. Believe me, I REALLY hate doing it, because I have never had this much fun in a conversation before, and I am afraid that if we stop now the moment will be lost. But a promise is a promise, and I don't like to be late. I am supposed to meet that scout for dinner."

Sarah looked disappointed but managed to rally quickly. "Yes, I get commitment, and it might be kind of important to your baseball future too, Mr. Howell. Yes, of course, I understand, and you had warned me beforehand, but I would be lying if I said that I didn't wish you could stay a little longer. We were really getting into some interesting topics, and I think you could teach me a few things about the brain that would inform my own faith beliefs. I hope we can continue this again soon."

"Oh, you bet. The sooner the better. But I think it will be good for me to process some of these thoughts and maybe I can come up with a better synthesis of what I believe in, which might add more to our next conversation."

Sarah noticed it was the third time in five minutes Charlie had used the word "process". And now "synthesis" too. She hoped he was not too married to the rigors of thinking, one of those guys who lived only in his head. She decided to let the thought drop. All she wanted to do after he left was dream about their next conversation.

"I can come by again tomorrow, if you want, Sarah."

The thought startled her for some reason.

"Yeah, that would be great. About the same time?"

"That works. See you then."

He rose, and she moved toward him, not sure what would happen.

"And good luck tonight with your scout."

"Thanks. I am not sure what we are going to talk about, but I it could be interesting. "

With that, Charlie pulled her close and kissed her on the cheek. It was a safe play. No point in making things awkward at this juncture. But as he moved away, Sarah reached up and caught his neck with her right hand, pulling his lips down to hers.

chapter 26

CHARLIE PULLED INTO the Houstons parking lot at 8:28. Bob Neal was waiting for him at the front door, and they were seated immediately. Charlie wondered about that, because he had never been seated right away at Houstons before, though admittedly he was not a regular customer there. Dr. Neal got down to business right away, and Charlie figured he was in the company of a real non-nonsense guy who put great value on his time.

"Charlie, as you know when you signed the waiver earlier in the year, we have been given access to your transcript, and frankly we are worried about something."

Charlie was a little taken aback but tried to remain nonchalant. "And what is that?"

"Well, we really like what we see on the field but frankly your grades are unbelievable and some people are concerned that you might just be a little too smart for professional baseball. As a career, I mean. We are afraid you might get bored—as you know, baseball is not rocket science, or I guess in your case I should say 'brain science'. There is also a school of thought in the organization, though neither Theo nor I is in that school, that athletes should not be thinkers, because thinkers tend to overanalyze rather than just play. I personally am not worried, because I have noticed over a number of years that the thing that really counts is a player's level of commitment to and passion for the game. I know because I was one of those guys who discovered that he just did not love it enough, and more importantly, I knew I was missing something else I wanted more. So that's what I want to know from you—how much do you love the game? How long will the passion last? What other ambitions do you have that we should know about now? We don't want to go wasting a second or third round pick on someone who can't wait to go to medical school, after he has scratched a small itch to play in the Show."

Charlie was listening, but then got quite distracted when he heard the words "second or third round pick". That sounded pretty definitive. That sounded really high and would certainly carry with it a significant signing bonus! He tried to contain himself and look reflective for a moment before responding.

"I understand, and I guess I should start by thanking you for the compliment—I never mind being thought of as a good thinker. And I won't lie to you, I do think a lot out there on the field. Sometimes I even think about things that don't relate to baseball, although Coach would tell you that I might have missed a sign once in my whole career at UCI, so it's not like my head is not in the game. Let me ask you, though, since you have a lot more experience, what do you think leads to overanalyzing and getting in your head too much? Is it a function of raw capacity, or some other phenomenon, psychological or neurophysiological?"

Bob Neal smiled. This was precisely why he personally had wanted to fly out and meet Charlie Howell. He had a sense that Charlie was something special, and already he was finding out why. For one, he liked the way Charlie thoughtfully dealt with his question, asking him one in return, in order to gain more information, perhaps even to mutually explore a topic that had plagued scouts for years. For another, the guy was clearly one bright kid, and Neal loved running into great minds, wherever he found them.

"Good question, Charlie. Let's order, and then I will see if I can give you an intelligent answer." Charlie asked for the grilled tuna, with Houston's famous garlic mashed potatoes. Neal had steak.

"First of all, Charlie, I see from your transcript that you have been taking a number of courses in neuroscience and cognitive sciences, so you may actually be able to enlighten me on some of the latest thinking. It's been seven years since I got my doctorate, and I mainly try to stay up with the psychology journals. But let me give you my psychologist viewpoint. I agree with you that it's probably not about capacity so much as need. Granted there are many people who have powerfully analytical brains, which tends to determine their way of looking at the world, but those who are prone to overanalyzing, whether they be ballplayers or lawyers, suffer from the need for control, in my opinion. Some-

133

where along the line, as children, they did not feel safe, or they did not feel that they were in control of their physical or emotional safety, so they adopted strategies for making sure they would always know what was going on, in order to control the situation. Any of that ring a bell for you?"

"It makes sense to me, if that's what you mean. And it's probably a straightforward enough theory to apply in assessing ballplayer's tendencies toward over analysis—or as I like to call it, "paralysis from analysis." But if you mean, do I think any of those syndromes might apply to me, no I don't think that rings a bell. Let me give you another thought, though."

"Please."

"Well, tell me if this is all very obvious to you already, but what if a person's predilections toward ways of thinking and dealing with life are all more or less determined by the way he or she is wired in the parts of the brain that generate working memory. In others words, I wonder if the way each of us thinks is simply a function of the way our brains are wired, how the millions of neural networks, circuits, and systems just happen to be connected with each other, which surely must vary from brain to brain."

Neal hesitated momentarily. "Yes, I suppose that makes sense, but unfortunately it does not provide us with a very useful tool to figure out in advance how a person may respond in certain environments, especially stressful ones. As you know, the field of neuroscience is a long way from really understanding how the brain works, not to mention being able to equate certain brain activities with particular thought processes."

"True, we are a very long way off, but we do have to start postulating some theories and focusing on how to falsify or prove them."

"It's an interesting approach, Charlie, and I think it reveals something important about you that helps me in my due diligence."

"What is that?"

"That you are a creative thinker. Maybe even a dreamer. Someone who thinks more in terms of asking questions than necessarily pursuing answers. We live in an Information Age, when many of the answers we might seek—though granted not so much in neuroscience—are readily available from that great source of group intelligence we call the Internet, but the real challenge of this age will be learning to ask the right questions. Your type is not inclined to over analyze what has happened in the past, which is what haunts the ballplayers we are leery of, those guys who can't let go of an 0 for 5, 2 error day for a week. I don't think you are like that, though I wouldn't be surprised if you spent some time in the dugout after a strikeout wondering why your mind was thinking a certain way instead of just focused on the pitcher's right hand as he released the ball."

"Touché. You must be very good at what you do."

Neal smiled graciously. "Well, I don't know. There is no science to figuring out how people will perform under pressure. But I would say that psychological profiling is the best tool I have in my bag today."

"You are probably right, but I bet you that won't be the case in fifteen to twenty years."

"I won't take that bet, and something tells me you might be the person whose article in the New England Journal of Medicine spells that out."

"That's a fun thought to play with."

"And speaking of playing, I know you guys don't have a game until next Wednesday, so I want you to fly back to Boston with me tomorrow and talk to Theo and the boys about money."

Charlie practically dropped his fork.

Neal knew Charlie was caught off guard and tried to add some levity. "That was almost an 'E-6'", he chuckled, alluding to the scoring notation for a shortstop's error. "I know it is short notice, and I didn't ask you about your course work obligations, or personal ones either."

Yes, personal obligations. Charlie wondered what Sarah's reaction would be. He thought she would just be happy for him, but she was still sick and in the hospital, and probably very much looking forward to seeing him the next day.

"Ah, I don't think that would be a problem, but I will have to check," Charlie quickly added. He couldn't imagine not going, nor was he entirely prepared to go. He needed time.

"Well, listen. You have my cell number. Call me before midnight and let me know. The flight is at 9:30 in the morning, out of Orange County, so we'll need to be organized this evening. I have a reservation for you, and we can get your return flight booked and buy the ticket at the airport tomorrow."

"Yes, sir. I mean, I just have to sort of get things organized, but I don't think I have anything that can't wait."

Neal knew what was going on and was satisfied with where they left it. It was a big step for any 21 year old, no matter how talented. "Boston's a little chilly this time of the year, so bring some warm clothes, although you won't be back there very long."

Charlie wondered if Coach knew about all this and tried to think back about his demeanor during the game that day. He guessed that Neal might have chatted with him after Charlie had left, just to make sure there were no important practice games scheduled for the next few days.

"How about dessert, Charlie, or does a guy like you keep to a strict diet?"

"No, sir. Not me. I love dessert."

"Good. That's another of my psychological profile leading indicators. But I am not sure about being called "sir".

They both chuckled and Neal motioned to the waiter.

chapter 27

By the time Charlie had reached the lot where Russ normally parked his car, all concerns he might have had about taking an unscheduled trip to Boston had vanished. And a few pluses had emerged. For one, he couldn't wait to see the look on Russ' face when he tossed him the keys, thanked him for use of the car, briefly described his interesting conversation with Sarah, and then casually asked for a lift to the airport at 8:00 in the morning. Of course, he would let Russ inquire as to where Charlie was off to and Charlie would casually explain that he had a little meeting with Theo he needed to attend. Just him and Theo. Russ certainly knew who Theo Epstein was, so saying it like that would elicit the appropriate "you are shitting me!!" response from Russ that Charlie would delight in. And then he imagined Russ telling the rest of the guys at practice the next day. Charlie's smile grew bigger with each passing image. But he still needed to check in with Coach and strategize some more about how to break the news to

Sarah. He didn't imagine she would be quite as excited as Russ.

Coach first. It was only just after 10:00 PM and he figured Coach would still be up, though Charlie suspected it wouldn't be long before he would call it a day.

"Coach, it's Charlie. Hope I am not calling too late."

"Close, Charlie, but no, it's fine. What's up?"

"I had dinner with Bob Neal tonight, the scout from the Red Sox."

"Yeah, I know. We chatted briefly after the game today."

Coach was either being very coy, or Charlie was going to have to do some work to get his permission.

"Well, I think they are pretty interested in me."

"That's what Neal said, yes."

"So what else did he say?"

"Not much. Just wanted to introduce himself and tell me what they thought about you. He wanted to make sure we didn't have any games in the next few days. Suppose he wanted to see another game if possible."

"Well, then, I guess he didn't tell you that they wanted me to fly to Boston tomorrow to meet with Theo Epstein." Charlie had tried to sound cool about it, but he suspected Coach wasn't buying.

"Yeah, now that you mention it. He kind of asked me if that was OK by me."

Charlie wished he was face to face with the coach, so he could figure out how much he was being played by the old guy. He always had gotten along well with Coach but was never sure if there wasn't a facet to the old man's character that was never revealed to any of the players, including his favorites, of which Charlie surely was one. Perhaps there was a side to Coach he didn't know, and which he would have to navigate carefully. *Or maybe the old buzzard is just pulling my leg!"*

"And?"

"And so it's fine with me, Charlie. That's great. Just don't talk to any agents. Like I have told all you guys a hundred times, you can't sign an agent before you are done playing ball here. And with you, I am sure I don't need to mention that you should have an agent before you sign ANYTHING with the Sox, or anyone else for that matter."

Charlie thought Coach was starting to sound cross. Maybe that was it. He had no use for scouts, because scouts always were trying to pressure kids, if they were any good, to come out early and forego graduation. Maybe Coach just hated this whole side of the game, because it could only screw up what he was trying to do, which was to win games and keep kids in school.

"Yeah, Coach. I know. I was paying attention all those times. No sweat."

"OK, then. Have yourself a good time. Say hi to Theo for me. And don't think you won't have to do your laps for missing practice."

Charlie knew the coach was just funning him on the last bit.

"Will do, Coach. Thanks."

He hoped it would go as well with Sarah, but decided he would handle that tomorrow from the airport.

chapter 28

CHARLIE CHECKED IN on the homework situation, waited a suitable length of time to call Neal back and confirm their flight time, and dropped the keys off with Russ. Russ reacted with predictable enthusiasm, though he actually said "holy shit, dude!" rather than "you are shitting me!" when Charlie told me about travel plans.

He also decided to write Sarah a long email before he went to bed, then call her the next morning to say goodbye. Charlie admitted to himself he was having fun getting to know Sarah but also found himself wondering if developing a romantic relationship really did involve as much strategy and forethought as he seemed to be generating lately.

After packing a small overnight bag, figuring he was fine wearing just a button down shirt and slacks to any meeting with Theo, he sat down to his computer.

Dear Sarah,
I hope you will forgive me for not coming to see you tomorrow, but the Red Sox want me to talk to them in Bos-

ton!! I just got back from dinner with the chief scout, and he wants us to be on a plane tomorrow morning at 9:30, so it does not look like I will be getting much sleep tonight!

I cannot tell you how much I enjoyed our conversation today, so because I am skipping out on you tomorrow, I want to see if we can keep it going by email for a couple of days. I actually like email, because it provides enough time to communicate thoughtfully but obviously allows for much quicker responses than snail mail. Anyway, I did have a few new thoughts, so I wanted to pass them along.

First, let me say thanks for all you shared with me about your spirituality. I learned a lot! Then I got to thinking about what might actually lead to my having a unique sense of myself and my spiritual connection to the Creator. It seems to me that if we have DNA that helps shape our unique physical characteristics and probably some element of our personality profiles as well, we might have a similar type of "spiritual DNA" that determines our tendencies to be open to relationship with the Creator and all the other aspects of spirituality you mentioned. I don't know much about this, but I read an interesting article once by Roger Penrose and Stuart Hameroff on the quantum computational aspects of mind and consciousness. They maintain that information can be encoded at a quantum level within the microtubules of the brain's neurons and that information could be embedded in these systems in an entirely different manner than information is managed by the brain's neurocomputational systems. (OK, maybe I will have to explain all that a bit more when I get back, but basically quantum computing is an entirely new way of manipulating information—instead of just using 'deci-

sion gates' of 1's and 0's, it uses all of the 32 potential quantum states of a 'quantum bit', or 'qubit', so it can perform multiple computations simultaneously and manipulate a lot more data, at a much faster rate than is possible with existing computational methodology.)

You said that the Creator has a Spirit dimension, right, and that Spirit is manifested energy? So if that is true, could not the Spirit of the Creator, as an energy source, somehow influence the content and mechanics of the brain's quantum computational systems? We are still learning about the nature and dynamics of energy at the quantum level, but it seems that the Creator would be able to energetically affect the quantum computational behavior of the brain, both in utero when we might say the "soul is formed" and throughout a person's life—what many people report, with great credibility, as their "encounters with God." If the Creator can reach across the dimensions of spacetime, could not that same Creator form an incarnated soul by influencing the way a brain is "pre-wired', using some sort of quantum information? Perhaps that is precisely what happens to give us what I have referred to as the "core consciousness" each of us brings with us into this world. I know this sounds a little far out, but I thought you might be intrigued by the notion, which I suppose you could call the neuroscience of how the Creator forms our "souls", or spiritual DNA.

BTW, even if our brains don't have any quantum computational capacities, the way in which synapses get wired together in neural networks, circuits, and systems greatly affects the way our individual brains work, so there is a very complex set of factors that goes into making up *your brain, and as a consequence, the way any individual brain is constructed is hard to map, not to mention that it is hard to predict what kind of mind might emerge from any given brain. Still, I find it interesting to think about why some, like you, seem so innately spiritual, and how that might have actually been wired into your brain in some way. What do you think?!?!*

Well, I have to get packed, so I will send this off. I will call from the airport to let you know for sure what is going on, in case you don't get this email right away, although I think you have your Blackberry right by your bed there!

Take care. Hope the reports from the doctor continue to improve and that you can get out of there soon. I will be thinking about you (don't know if I am any good at praying).

Charlie

Charlie scanned his email again and thought twice about sending it. It sounded a bit academic and cryptic, but he decided to send it anyway. It would certainly give her something to chew on while he was away, and he wanted to uphold his end of the conversation! He hit the Send button and switched off his computer.

chapter 29

"UNITED FLIGHT 57 is now in its final boarding at gate 4."

Charlie was getting a little frantic. Sarah still had not returned his call from 45 minutes ago, and in 15 minutes he would have to turn his cell phone off.

Why am I so stressed to talk to her? It's not like we are even dating. I guess I just wanted to share the excitement of the trip, and the Red Sox interest. Geez, I haven't even called my parents, and here I am worrying about hearing from Sarah.

"C'mon, Charlie, let's board." Neal had appeared from nowhere, instantly pulling Charlie out of the little conversation he was having with himself, in a seemingly endless feedback loop of speculation and agitation.

Charlie stepped into the boarding line just as his cell phone rang, playing the tune of Sweet Caroline, which Charlie knew to be a recently adopted theme of the Sox and which he had downloaded the night before. Neal turned, clearly impressed.

"Nice touch. But you won't win any points with Theo, because you better have it turned off during your meeting!"

The phone kept ringing, and if it was Sarah, the last thing Charlie wanted was Neal close by, eavesdropping.

"Duly noted, Bob. Excuse me. I will catch up with you."

Charlie ducked out of line and opened the phone. "Hello."

"Hi, Charlie, it's Sarah. I just got your message! When did you call?"

"Almost an hour ago. We're boarding the flight right now, so I won't have much time, but I am really glad you caught me. Did you get my email?"

"I did. Wow, that's fantastic. Going to Boston to talk with the Red Sox. Congratulations!"

"Thanks. I really wanted to talk to you too, though. I feel bad about not being able to come to the hospital today."

"That's sweet, Charlie, but don't worry, I will be fine. And you did hold up your end of the promise in one sense by sending me that email. It may take me a couple of days just to digest it, so you may be back before I can even respond!"

"I am glad you liked it. It's just something that came to me, so it may not be a very plausible approach. But I really look forward to hearing your thoughts."

"OK, I will go to work on it. There's not much else to do down here."

Charlie thought the last comment sounded like a tongue in cheek ploy for sympathy, but it would be too risky to call her bluff and have it backfire on him, so he played it safe.

"I will let you know when I am coming back and definitely will come see you as soon as I have a chance."

"I'll be waiting."

"Take care, Sarah."

"And you have a safe flight, Charlie."

"Thanks. Bye."

"Bye. Oh, and Charlie?"

"Yeah?"

"I like Boston."

Charlie didn't know what to say. The comment sounded both purposeful and suggestive, but they didn't really have that type of relationship. At least not yet. Again, Charlie decided to deftly deflect the comment.

"Great. I will bring you back something."

"Bye."

"Bye."

chapter 30

HAVING NOT GOTTEN a full night's rest, Charlie had originally planned to sleep on the flight to Boston, though he quickly discovered when he arrived at the airport that the flight was connecting in Chicago, which would break up any chance of a long snooze. But he soon discovered that he and Neal had a number of similar intellectual interests, so they spent the entire four hour flight to O'Hare talking about life, baseball, and neuroscience. As the plane started its decent, Neal offered a few parting thoughts.

"Charlie, I know it sounds trite, but whatever you do, always do it because you are being true to yourself. Your real self, not the self that your parents might have envisioned for you, the person your girlfriend, wife, or friends want you to be. *Your* self, the self that only you could ever really know or comprehend. It takes a great deal of self-examination, introspection, and courage, because by definition you are on that journey alone, always deciding if what you are doing is really who you are and what you are meant to be about, but it is worth it. And along the way, you will meet people who will encourage you, even if they don't understand completely what you are up to. When I decided to leave baseball, I was completely at peace with my decision. There was something else calling me, and I knew it was right. You have a bright future ahead of you, perhaps in a couple of different of fields—no pun intended—and I suspect it will be important for you to keep track of why you are choosing to do something, from the very beginning."

Charlie was transfixed. His first thought was that this was precisely the kind of advice that he had missed growing up without a father. He somehow knew it was essential to have a good mentor in one's life, and he wondered if Bob Neal might turn out to be just such a person.

"Thanks, Bob. I will certainly remember that. I guess I have always had a strong sense of myself and who I am, but I know that life, and the choices I have in life, will start to get more complicated. Choosing to play baseball at UCI while looking around at what I would enjoy studying is one thing, but making career choices and getting the timing right is quite another."

Neal nodded appreciatively. "Obviously, I want you to come play for the Sox, but honestly I would not be doing you or my employer any favors if I blindly encouraged you to think about nothing but baseball, especially if I suspect it would not be the best thing for you. Remember, it's not like you are going to just walk into the lineup at Fenway next spring. It can be a long slug to the Big Leagues, even for the talented players. Nor I am saying you ought to decide in advance how many years you are going to play before you even start. None of us, Theo included, can predict with complete accuracy how productive a player is going to be, or even how long he is going to be able to play. Granted, football is physically demanding in a different way than baseball, but look at a guy like Barry Sanders, who could have gone on a lot longer but who just decided, for reasons that only he understands, just to stop at a certain point."

Charlie looked at Neal thoughtfully, who was clearly in a very philosophical mood. "This may sound obvious to you too, Charlie, but life is more complicated and complex than you can possibly imagine at your age. Now all you worry about are curveballs, studies, and women. It may occasionally seem overwhelming, but believe me, for someone of your talent, it will only get harder. You will feel pulled in more than more direction and have times when you just feel there are not enough hours in the day to keep everyone in your life happy. And life will throw you a curveball or two before long, maybe even a couple of nasty splitters as well, if you know what I mean. I don't mean to sound like a downer, but I just want to give you a glimpse of what your life as a Major Leaguer will look like. Of course, there will be tremendous numbers of thrills too."

Charlie somehow knew this was true, though as Neal had indicated, he could not really appreciate it fully from his current perspective. But Charlie had the kind of life smarts that told him when he was receiving wise advice, which could be stored away and retrieved when appropriate. He nodded as Neal continued.

"Not that you have to do anything about that now, but just keep it in the back of your mind. I wish someone had told me that when I was your age, so I am telling you now. And trust me, there will be a point in your life when you remember this, when you look back on your life and see how the accumulated set of experiences that were uniquely yours led up to your becoming your own person, with a particular capacity, fully known and understood only by you, to make a contribution to this world, to make it a better place. For me, I just came to that stage last year, when I spent some time wondering what might have been if I had continued in baseball. I traced back a whole series of events that took place after I hung up my spikes, and now I see how it all led me right into this job, which allows me to pass on some experience to guys like you, to make sure they are really grounded when they come into our organization, to make sure they are going to be good citizens of the Boston community once they make it here. That makes me feel good about what I do and who I am."

Charlie was starting to become really impressed with the Sox culture and attitudes towards its players. He found himself wondering if perhaps this was even part of a well designed recruiting strategy. But Neal seemed really sincere and genuinely interested in Charlie, regardless of what happened in his upcoming discussions with Theo and what ultimately unfolded in the draft.

The plane bumped through a few clouds, causing Charlie to straighten up in his seat. He hadn't flown so much that the occasional patch of rough air couldn't still capture the full attention of his brain and its ever vigilant early warning systems. He was sure Neal had noticed and took the opportunity to acknowledge his innocence.

"I guess there are a lot of things I still haven't experienced."

"Yeah, but trust me, flying is among of the easiest parts of the job."

"Then what did *you* find difficult? What was the hardest thing for you to adjust to after you got drafted?"

"The same thing that made me decide to leave—undeniable mediocrity. As long as I still felt I had the potential to be an All Star, the game was fun and therefore worth playing. I always believed I was put on this earth for a distinct purpose, a purpose that I would know and understand by how well my skills and interests were manifested in the pursuit of that purpose. At the outset, I was willing to consider that baseball, and all the attendant opportunities that would open up if I were successful, was the source of just such a purpose. But after three years in the minors, and a full season in Major League Baseball, it was pretty clear in my mind that I would never be any more than a .275 hitter and frankly, by then I was pretty sure there was something else that would serve as a better platform for my talents and passions."

Charlie smiled. "Mediocre is not my ambition either, but by the same token I don't feel driven to greatness; in fact, I don't even necessarily feel greatness anywhere in me. I simply want to do something that I am passionate about and which is expressive of who I am. I think it was Emerson who said God expected that much of us, so I should aspire at least to that."

"Well said. Always remember that. But for the short term, most especially your conversation with Theo tomorrow, assume that God wants you to be the best baseball player who ever lived."

"I could think of worse ways to spend one's life."

"You wouldn't starve, that much is true."

chapter 31

THE CITY LOOMED below, cold and grey, as they came in over the new Convention Center, then crossed the harbor on their approach to runway 17 at Boston's Logan airport. Charlie didn't think it looked like a particularly dreary day, but that might just have been because of how eager he was to meet Theo. Off to the left, tucked behind the Prudential Center, the lights of Fenway burned in the gathering gloom, and Neal quickly pointed them out to Charlie before they touched down. It was still Spring Training, so there was no game going on there, but it helped fuel Charlie's sense of anticipation.

They grabbed a cab and made to Yawkey Way in less than 20 minutes. When the finally entered Fenway, Charlie was immediately impressed by the presence of the Green Monster and how much it seemed to define the intimate confines of the stadium. Later, he was equally surprised at how modest Theo's office was. It looked more like a command bunker than a place where the Senior Vice President and General Manager might entertain big time agents and their sought after players. Maybe those meetings were conducted elsewhere. And maybe this was effectively a command bunker after all, a secure location where Theo and his staff could pour over stats and endless reports on players, in a never ending effort to stay ahead of the market, especially the complicated free agent market. The one thing that did not surprise Charlie was Theo's appearance and demeanor. Neal had briefed him well, alerting him to his seeming aloofness, which in actuality was nothing more than a protective mask for his reserved, even shy, nature.

Theo seemed to emerge from a hidden alcove just as Charlie and Neal walked through the door.

"Bob, good to see you. Hope the flight was uneventful."

"Yes, fine, thanks, Theo. Theo, this is Charlie Howell."

"Charlie. Good to finally meet you. We have been hearing great things."

"Thank you, sir. It's a pleasure to meet you."

Charlie noticed he had been addressing everyone as "sir" in the last 24 hours. Theo was only 12 years older than Charlie, but somehow it didn't feel that strange calling him "sir". After all, the guy had already won a World Series.

"Have a seat. The boys and I were actually just going over the draft charts this morning. We put you up on the board as a third rounder."

Neal smiled, mostly to himself. Theo was all business. Why waste time on pleasantries.

Charlie thought Theo expected a response.

"That sounds pretty high. Just out of curiosity who do you have in front of me?"

Theo seemed to have expected the question.

"Jarrett from Long Beach and Sanchez from Texas. You must know Jarrett, right?"

"Oh, yes. He's got a curve ball that's hard to for-get."

"Well, maybe you won't have to face him any more, except in intersquad games. We certainly hope that you both end up playing for the fans of Red Sox Nation."

"It would be a dream come true for me, I know that." For some reason, an image of Sarah and her mom, sitting in the players' seats at Fenway, leapt into Charlie's mind."Glad to hear that Charlie. Hopefully that will make contract negotiations go smoothly."

Even Neal had not expected Theo to jump into the fray that quickly, but there seemed to be other things on his mind, and he was proceeding with his usual dispatch. Charlie didn't seem to mind, and soon Neal found out why.

"Well, I hope so, sir. Of course, I don't even have an agent yet, but I favor expedition myself, so that is what I will be pushing."

Theo looked at Neal, knowing full well that he had coached Charlie about a few things and wondered if he had even talked with him about agents. Some-times clubs liked to steer their prospects toward agents like Jerry Kapstein, with whom the Red Sox had always been able to do business, but it was a tricky area, and

Theo knew Neal was smart enough to stay out of providing any direct advice on the matter.

Theo decided to start testing the waters. "When you do get an agent, Charlie, you can tell him that we are thinking about a three year deal, with a signing bonus of around $500,000."

Charlie had done his homework and was ready. He smiled gratefully but suggested little other emotion.

"That sounds pretty good to a starving college student". Charlie was pretty sure Theo understood he was neither starving nor likely to tip his hand at this point. Better just leave it until draft time. Anyway, Theo had gotten what he was looking for, which was a good read on Charlie's integrity. That, together with the report Neal had given him early that morning before he boarded the flight from Orange County, in which he basically had related how sharp Charlie was, was all Theo needed to make his draft decision. He had to get back to other work.

"Charlie, I apologize but I have to get back to Lucchino and Henry on something, but I am very pleased to have met you and look forward to seeing you again after the draft. You are definitely high on our list. Bob, how about taking Charlie around the rest of the facility. And I think Larry said he wanted to say hello as well."

"Will do, Theo, but we'll make it quick. I think I have a hungry athlete on my hands and I bet there are a couple of joints down in the North End he would enjoy."

"I have no doubt that *you* know where they are, Bob. Enjoy the rest of your time in Boston, Charlie. You are in capable hands on that score."

"Thank you, sir. It was a pleasure meeting you, and I am sure I will look forward to the draft even more now. Oh, I almost forgot. Could you do me a big favor?" Charlie suddenly panicked when he realized he did not know how exactly how to word the request. He decided he could take a little liberty with the truth in characterizing Sarah's allegiance to the Red Sox Nation, especially since her mother was such a big fan.

"A friend of mine is in the hospital back home, and both she and her mother are huge Sox fans. I wonder if you could sign a couple of hats or something for me."

"Sure, no problem. I will have them sent up to Larry's office, and you can pick them up before you leave."

"Thanks, I really appreciate that. They will be thrilled."

chapter 32

AFTER TOURING THE byzantine interior of Fenway Park and walking around the outfield warning track, stopping to touch the Green Monster, as if it were some sort of Wailing Wall, Charlie spent a pleasant fifteen minutes with the Red Sox President, Larry Lucchino. Well educated and conversationally gifted, Lucchino managed to engage Charlie in a brief discussion about psychology and his theories about what types of profiles made for good baseball players. Charlie wasn't sure if he was supposed to volunteer his own self profile but decided against it. He also decided not to offer any of his own theories about the nature of the human mind, though he deemed them more useful than psychology in helping to explain what motivates people to behave as they do.

Following a quick beer at the Bull & Finch, the famous Boston bar upon which the TV show *Cheers* had been styled, Charlie and Bob Neal headed to the North End for some quintessential Italian cuisine. The conversation was light, mostly around other Red Sox prospects, the organization's draft philosophy, and the club's chances in the upcoming season. Before long, Charlie was feeling weary and Neal was looking forward to seeing his wife, so they made it an early evening, and Neal dropped Charlie off at the nearby Sheraton Long Warf. Neal promised to stay in touch, and Charlie once again got the sense that Neal had taken a real interest in him, as a person, not just a player.

Charlie's room had a nice view of the harbor and Logan airport behind it, so he sat down at the desk near the window and spent a few moments reflecting on the last 24 hours' events. His thoughts eventually turned to Sarah, and he silently hoped (*was it a prayer?*) that she was recovering fully. The room was wired for Web access, so Charlie pulled out his laptop and began to compose an email.

Dear Sarah,

Sitting here in my hotel room overlooking Boston Harbor. Had a pleasant and informative visit to Fenway Park, where I met both Theo and Larry Lucchino, the Red Sox President. And oh, I got you and your mom souvenirs as well. Think your mom will be particularly thrilled, but don't tell her about it.

It looks like I will be back Monday around noon. They want me to take a battery of tests tomorrow. Shouldn't be too difficult, then I will have some time in the afternoon I suspect to just wander on my own. Hope the weather holds.

I am sorry about not being out there to cheer you up. I am sure you are getting tired of being in the hospital.

But I am looking forward to picking up our conversation. I thought about a few other things during the flight here today. Bob Neal—he's the head scout who came out to California and flew back with me—is an ex-player and a fascinating guy. We had a long talk on the plane, and he told me about his career and decision to quit when he was still just 27. He had some great insights about what is important in life, so maybe I will relate some of what he told to you later as well.

Well, I am pretty beat, so I think I will log off. Take care. Charlie.

Charlie logged off and put his laptop away. The harbor was dark and quiet. Time to watch a few minutes of ESPN. It was always a good way to end the day. Harmless entertainment, though perhaps someday, when Charlie was watching himself on an ESPN highlight film, he might feel differently.

chapter 33

FOR LATE MARCH in Boston, when it can be cruelly cold just as it seems winter should be over, it seemed a pleasant morning. Not being used to East Coast time, Charlie rose late and enjoyed a leisurely breakfast, before heading up to Faneuil Hall Market to do some sightseeing. From there, he wandered over to the Commons, then down to the Charles River. A few hearty sailors had taken to the water, but they were clearly outnumbered by rowers, who obviously were used to braving the chilly weather during the late fall and early spring.

The tests he had taken the day before at Fenway were mostly physical, though there was a Meyers Briggs profile and a battery of other psychological tests. He had no problem with any of them. So far it had been a very enjoyable and successful trip.

By mid afternoon Charlie was hungry again, so he headed back to Faneuil Hall's food court. The mild temperatures had brought more than a few Bostonians out to enjoy the fresh air, so a few street artists had decided there was enough money to be made. One had just started his routine, which amounted to different types of juggling and making fun of passersby, when Charlie arrived. He made sure to stay on the perimeter of the crowd, so he would not fall victim to any of the performer's pranks.

By 4 PM, Charlie was back in his room, realizing that he missed southern California. It wasn't that Boston was not interesting, but it just wasn't California. He picked up the phone and called both United and Delta to check on the next available flights and discovered he could be home by 8:45 if he could make the 5:15 flight. It only took him 4 minutes to pack and by 4:20 he was on the water taxi to Logan. He made the flight with 15 minutes to spare.

chapter 34

SARAH TRIED TO pretend that it was a regular visit from a good friend, but the combination of her restlessness from having to stay in the hospital and some still un-identified sense of excitement she was feeling at the mere thought of Charlie Howell was making it difficult. She had received Charlie's text message late Sunday evening, telling her that he would be arriving later that night and would come to see her the next day. Now it was already 10 AM on Monday morning, and she had not heard from him. The knock on the door surprised her. And of course, that was just what Charlie had want-ed.

To be sure, she was surprised but not unprepared. She had dressed in jeans and a teal silk chemise, bare on the shoulders, no bra. Its color was designed to draw immediate attention to her green eyes, though likely that would not be the first place most men would look, especially after she had decided to leave the bra out of the equation. She hoped her mother wouldn't notice but knew that wasn't likely. On the other hand, she knew Charlie would, and that was very much the point.

When he entered, Charlie not only noticed but suddenly seemed the more surprised of the two. He hesitated as he approached, seemingly disarmed. In his mind's eye, he had visualized their meeting again, and he had planned to give her a generous and enthusiastic hug. Now, it was almost as though her beauty and the delicate magnificence of her barely concealed breasts made her appear too precious to touch, a china doll too exquisite to handle.

Having recovered her composure, Sarah now restrained herself and maintained her position in front of the window. Though she wanted desperately to run up and embrace him, even kiss him, she would let him come to her, because she would learn more that way. She would be able to read the subtle clues he would give her, without his even knowing, about what he was feeling, and more than anything, she wanted to know that. During his brief trip to Boston, Sarah had come to realize how much she missed him, felt connected to him, and wanted to know him better. *C'mon, Charlie, get your cute little rear over here and kiss me!!*

Though it seemed like an eternity to Sarah, Charlie's hesitation lifted almost immediately, and he moved swiftly toward her. Maybe it was some sort of electro-chemical connection that suddenly started to flow as soon as he had entered the room. And maybe it was just his hormones taking over. Whatever it was, it was powerful, and he almost knocked Sarah over with his embrace. When they finally regained their balance, literally and figuratively, he slowed down his delivery and kissed her on the lips. She didn't let go for a long time.

By the time she released her arms from around his neck and slid down off his torso, Charlie realized how good it had felt to have the warmth of her breast on his chest and was having trouble containing his sexual desire. He turned at a 45 degree angle from her, hoping she wouldn't notice. Of course she had, but she pretended not to. And in truth she was much more interested in the gathering sensation she felt that she was in some way coming home to a place that had been a very distant memory. There seemed to be a spiritual quality to what she was feeling. She grabbed his hand, wanting to hold on to both the feeling and her sense of deep connection to him.

"I missed you, Charlie. I am glad you are safely back."

"Me too. That's why I grabbed an earlier flight. How are you? Any news from the doctor?"

"Yes, in fact, he said I could go home today, so your timing is impeccable."

"That's fantastic, Sarah. I am really happy for you. And I bet your mom is thrilled. Is she still here? And what did the doctor say?"

Ann Wilson appeared, seemingly out of nowhere.

"Yes, I am still here. And yes, I am thrilled. Nice to see you again, Charlie. I understand you have had a pretty exciting weekend yourself. How are my boys doing back at Fenway?"

"Indeed I did. Met with both Theo and Lucchino. And I thought you might appreciate a little souvenir."

Charlie reached into a large white plastic bag and drew out one of the caps, holding the bill forward as he presented it to Ann Wilson, with almost as much ceremony and deference as a Japanese businessman presenting his business card. He wanted to make sure she saw Theo's signature, which had been placed on the inside of the bill, so he turned the cap upside down just before he handed it to her. She reached for it, and gasped when she understood.

"Oh my goodness, you even got Theo to sign it! Did you know, he never signs autographs? Never. I can't believe it. You met Theo. What was he like?"

Sarah couldn't really remember seeing her mother like this before.

"Mom, you're acting as bad as a Timberlake groupie."

"Well, I wouldn't know about that dear, but this is Theo we are talking about. You remember him, the guy who broke the Curse of the Bambino? The guy who brought a world championship to the Red Sox after 86 years of futility?"

Sarah smiled. "OK, OK. Now before you embarrass me completely in front of Charlie—"

"Here, Sarah, Theo signed this one too."

As Charlie turned Sarah's cap upside down, he noticed for the first time that an envelope had been stuck in it. It had Sarah's name on it. Sarah saw it, ignored Theo's scrawl on the underside of the bill, and reached for the envelope, her mind racing.

"And what's this? Charlie."

"I don't know. I didn't notice it when I stuck them in the bag in Boston. I just looked at one of the caps to see if Theo had signed them, and the envelope must have been in the second one."

Sarah started to rip at the corners of the envelope, as Charlie tried to sort out what it might be. He hadn't remembered even mentioning Sarah's name to anyone at Fenway. Sarah had removed the card, embossed with the Red Sox logo and the simple lettering, in italics, *"Larry Lucchino, President and CEO"*

"It's from the Red Sox president. "Hope you get well soon. Larry Lucchino."

Charlie squirmed. *Did I really tell him about Sarah? What is she going to think I told him?*

"That's really sweet. How did he know?"

"Honestly, Sarah, I am not sure. I had a great conversation with the scout, Bob Neal, on the flight to Boston, and I must have mentioned your illness to him. Not much detail of course. They are an amazing organization that way. Really on the ball, so to speak. And maybe that explains why Theo was so happy to provide the autograph, especially if Ann is right that he never gives autographs. Anyway, I am glad you are excited."

"Of course. Why wouldn't I?"

As she spoke, Sarah glanced over at her mom, who seemed to be paying particularly keen attention.

"I don't know. I thought maybe you would be upset that I had shared your condition with a virtual stranger."

"Don't be silly. As you say, I am sure you didn't tell them I was your fiancé or anything, or that I had some mysterious heart disease. I think it's sweet you were worried about me enough to have it in your consciousness when you were talking with this Bob Neal guy."

Charlie noticed that Ann Wilson was now looking at him like he was some kind of returning combat hero. "Well, I think it's sweet too, Charlie," she said. "And I am even more of a Sox fan now than I ever was. Wait till I tell Frank. Might even convert him, finally."

Charlie said a silent thanks to Lucchino. He would remember the gesture if he ever ended up sitting down with him in contract negotiations, and he figured that was probably precisely what Lucchino was thinking too, but it didn't bother him. Business is business. Baseball is business. His mind finally wandered back into the room.

"Well, then, I think it was sweet of him too. Guess that says a lot about the organization. Hey, Sarah, you still haven't told me what the doctor said."

"He basically said I would be fine. They will be able to tell better in 3 months whether there was any long term damage to the heart, but he is optimistic. He wants to keep an eye on me for the next couple of weeks but expects that after that I can resume my normal activities. Then a couple of weeks after I go back to exercising regularly, he wants to take another look. All in all, I guess I am a lucky girl."

Ann Wilson spoke first.

"I would certainly say so."

"Yeah, that is good news, Sarah." Charlie moved forward and gave her a gentle hug, given that her mom was now in the room and surely had noticed by now how her daughter was dressed. Sarah took the opportunity to grab his hand as he released his embrace. She held on, leading him to the door. No doubt it was a silent signal to her mom that Charlie was officially no longer just a friend.

"Well, let's go see about getting me sprung from this place, then."

Charlie instinctively looked at Ann, who smiled as if she had just gained a son-in-law and a star shortstop for her beloved Red Sox in the same transaction. She wondered whether now that Theo had signed a baseball cap for her she could call him up and suggest that he move Charlie up a round on their draft selection board. Of course she wouldn't, but she entertained herself thinking about it.

chapter 35

"IT'S SIMPLY A function of the way the brain forms, Sarah. As human beings, we are so much a product of our minds, and our minds are basically the end result of a very complex synaptic system inside our brains, supported of course by the body and all the biochemistry it supplies to or catalyzes in the brain. So that's why I say that the human mind 'emerges' from the functioning of the brain."

The UCI baseball season had ended two days earlier, after Cal State Fullerton beat them in the College World Series regional qualifying tournament. Charlie had been named the tournament MVP, but that had been small consolation, since he had hoped that in his last season he might finally make it into the World Series. Sarah was trying her best to think of ways to help him through his disappointment and had suggested a picnic at Crystal Cove. School had been over for two weeks, but Sarah wanted to stay around campus to spend time with Charlie, when he wasn't playing baseball. Her scare from the virus had changed some of her priorities, and though the doctor had done his best to assure her she would live a long and healthy life, there was still a different sense of urgency about her now. As they walked the long beach at Crystal Cove and gazed out at the Pacific Ocean on another spectacular May day in southern California, the conversation had become increasingly intense. Sarah listened to Charlie with rapt attention.

"As I said in our earlier conversation, we all are born with a core consciousness that is wired into our brains. There is a great deal of genetic differentiation and pure random development in the way our brains are formed, which guarantees that each human brain has its own unique characteristics, but there are some aspects of human consciousness that are common to all people and therefore commonly architected in our brains' synaptic connections. I doubt that we will ever figure out how it all works—can you imagine the scope of the whole system? I mean, you start with the notion that when our brains are fully developed, there may be as many as 40 *quadrillion*—that's 40 with 16 zeros—possible synaptic combinations that can be formed from the hundred billion or so neurons in our brains. And when you consider how different all of those possible combinations might be formed differently in each person, you begin to see how and why the subjective experience of our moment to moment thoughts, our consciousness of being alive, and our exercise of free will must be not just unique, but virtually untraceable neurologically."

Charlie seemed as though he could go on forever describing the intricacies of the brain and the mind, but it was Sarah who needed the break.

"Slow down, cowboy. You may not need to take a breath but I do. You're hurting *my brain!*"

"Actually, that's not surprising, because the brain is a very efficient machine, and since most of this is well etched in my neural networks, it does not take much energy to retrieve it. You, on the other hand, are having to process the information, synthesize, and store it. It takes a lot of energy to do that."

"Amazing. Just wind him up and watch him go." Her look was sardonic but playful, so Charlie played along, not wanting to give her the satisfaction of landing the only jab.

"It's true, you know, you can basically wind up the brain and let it go. In fact, did you know that all of your synapses are in a constant state of oscillation, awaiting some stimulus to engage them? It's called "long term potentiation", and it's ultimately the reason that we get stuck in our ways, don't want to alter our belief systems, and develop our psychological expectations. Our brains are always running, always sitting there *expecting* to process the type of stimuli it is already familiar with, even though life itself does not work that way. Obviously, it's a good strategy for the brain, because it makes for greater efficiency and allows it to conserve energy, but the problem comes when a set of expectations is not met. Which reminds me—"

"Charlie, seriously, can we take a little break from this stuff?"

Sarah's tone of voice, which was somewhat less playful and more insistent this time, seemed to startle Charlie. Sarah noticed that he even looked somewhat hurt.

"C'mon, let's just sit here for a moment and watch the surf. I am actually really intrigued by all this, but I need a second to absorb it, synthesize it, and think about one aspect in particular that I want to ask you about. OK?"

"Sure."

Charlie wasn't exactly pouting, but he also did not know exactly what to do with the time out Sarah needed. He was in full teaching mode, and it was not like he was suddenly just going to turn a switch and sit there with nothing to do. He stared out at the ocean, putting a mental bookmark in the information flow he had been sharing with Sarah and sat there, waiting for her.

After a few minutes, Sarah stood up and grabbed his hand.

"Ok, so tell me more about this core consciousness we all have?"

This, more than anything else, was the part of Sarah Wilson Charlie loved the most. She had such great range. More than just range in the sense that shortstops had to have it, which involved the ability to cover lots of ground. No, Sarah Wilson's range was functional—her personality, intellect, and interests were seemingly always in flux. You just had to give her time to make adjustments, find new capacity, whatever it was, but she would always rise to the occasion.

"So, Charlie, do you remember where we left off?"

"Of course, why?"

"Well, for a moment, you just seemed somewhere else, as though you were trying to remember something."

"Actually, I was thinking about something else—about what great psychological and intellectual range you have and how much I love that."

Sarah's face became flushed. "Really?"

"Yes, really, Sarah." Charlie brought her closer to him. "You are a gem, and there is so much about you that I love, it's hard to know where to start."

Sarah smiled, not really sure of what she wanted to say. Over the last month, she had been spending a great deal of time with Charlie and certainly was getting an idea of how he felt about her, but he had not expressed any specific feelings. She decided to draw him out.

"I wouldn't mind if you gave it a go."

"Well, for starters, I love the way you make me feel when I am with you. I guess I think that must be pretty important if you want to spend a lot of time with someone. You seem to be interested in whatever is on my mind, which as you know can be considerable these days. And you seem to believe in me, in all my little theories and ideas, and my skills. You make me feel that you believe I have what it takes, whatever that might be, and I don't think a guy could want more than that."

Sarah started getting teary, and there was a sensation welling up inside her she could not put words to. Charlie noticed and stopped walking, pulling her close.

"Oh, Charlie. It's true. I do believe in you, more than you can imagine."

Tears were streaking down her cheeks, and she made no attempt to stop either the tears or the thoughts and emotions that were generating them. It was the last thing either of them said to each other for the next few minutes, and when the moment had passed, neither of them seemed ready to go back to their previous conversation.

chapter 36

AFTER THEY FINISHED their picnic lunch of hummus, apples, cheese, and an entire baguette, Charlie and Sarah retired to a section of shade under the cliffs that rose steeply off the beach, some fifty yards from the water's edge. Charlie thought about lying down and trying to relax, but it was Sarah who initiated a return to their earlier conversation, with a different air of intentionality.

"Charlie, I have been thinking about something. I need you to explain the consciousness piece again. But I think I cut you off before you were finished telling me why we have such different brains and how that affects the ways our minds work, especially with respect to consciousness."

"Sure. Well, as I was saying, our brain architectures are so different to begin with, then you add to that a certain randomness about the way all the synapses come together, it's small wonder all of our perspectives on, and experiences of, life are different. On top of that, in any moment to moment snapshot of what is going on in our brains, we have to factor in the impact of bio-chemistry, which is significant. I don't even understand all the complexities of how neurotransmitters work with respect to the inner mechanics of synaptic events and other interneuronal activity, but I can tell you that a great deal of what actually goes on in the brain is af-fected by what hormones, peptides, and amines your body has been producing, or what types of drugs your body has been ingesting, since they either produce or otherwise alter the performance of some 40 odd dif-ferent neurotransmitters that drive the efficiency and effectiveness of your brain's synaptic activity."

"That does sound complicated. So how is all that relate to consciousness?"

"First I must tell you that there is a wide range of thought on the nature and substance of human con-sciousness, among philosophers, physicists, behavioral scientists, and neuroscientists, who even among them-selves hold widely divergent views. But as best I can fig-ure out, there are what I would call three basic sources of consciousness and five fundamental manifestations. First you have the consciousness that is embedded in your soul and which you bring into the world with you, which in earlier conversations I referred to as part of 'core consciousness'—who knows exactly how we de-velop it, maybe it comes from the universal intelligence that underlies a self-organizing universe—I guess what you would call 'divine intelligence'. I confess that I don't understand much about all that."

"Then there is the moment to moment conscious-ness generated by the normal function of the brain as it processes never ending streams of stimuli, which I alluded to earlier as 'access consciousness'—that obviously is sourced entirely inside the brain and is very mechanical."

"Finally, there is the consciousness that invades our minds from the very complex dynamics of memetics—memes are units of self-organizing information in human culture, and they necessarily use the human brain as an agent of replication and perpetuation."

"Whoa, partner, stop right there! Since we already talked about the soul thing—and I think you mentioned the spiritual DNA framework for that—I can follow that, and I have sort of followed your neurospeak, but what the heck are 'memes' and 'memetics'"?!

"Yeah, I know, more funny terms. Memetics basically represent the dynamics by which "memes" perpetuate themselves. "Memes" was a term coined by that famous atheist and Neo-Darwinist Richard Dawkins, who wanted to conceptualize a unit of culture—an idea or bit of information, if you will—and speculate on how such units of culture could be passed on from generation to generation, just like the information contained in genes. So, for example, in the United States, some prominent memes are freedom of speech and capitalism, and if you think about it, those ideas or concepts not only have a huge influence on our collective thinking in this country, they are the types of concepts that most of us grow up embracing without really thinking about it. So from that sense, it seems Dawkins has a good point, and you can begin to see how subconsciously embracing our pervading cultural memes might seep into—and partially define—a person's consciousness. Obviously, if you grew up in the U.S., the daughter of a fifth generation American, you will have embedded in your mind a different set of memes and a therefore a different consciousness than would, for example, an immigrant from Yemen."

"Cool theory. OK, so those are the three sources. What are the five manifestations?"

"Well, the first of the five would be the way you manifest generally, as a function of your personality, desires, belief systems, and what not. Its source could be the core consciousness of the soul or some significant experiences in life, most likely in the formative years of your life. This type of consciousness has many levels and aspects to it. You can have angst about certain domains of your life, like relationships. Or you can carry a fundamental anger about something, like the way people treat each other so harshly."

"The second manifestation would be what I call extended consciousness. The brain is a very complex system, which generates 'emergent properties', including what we call mind, ego, personality, and the like. One of the brain's key functions is recognizing, comparing, and cataloguing objects in its environment, and that includes life experiences as well. It is that function which, over time, eventually generates in the mind the emergent property that I call the 'autobiographical self'. It just seems to me that once that sense of autobiographical self emerges, a person's consciousness gains new dimensionality or context. With me, for example, I feel my consciousness has evolved in a specific way once I became a serious student and baseball player, gained the respect of my teammates, and began to see myself as a leader of sorts."

"The third manifestation is sourced in 'access consciousness' and simply depends on what is unique about the wiring and operation of your brain. As I mentioned earlier, I believe that brain biochemistry is particularly relevant here. The more we discover about diseases such as Alzheimer's, conditions like depression, and even every day moods, the more clear it is that neurotransmitters like serotonin and dopamine not only affect brain performance but define a person's ability to be aware of or have 'access' to certain information, feelings, or capacities. No question about it, brain biochemistry not only affects mood but consciousness."

Sarah held up her hand. "Good. But I have a question that has been brewing in my mind, Charlie."

Charlie sat up expectantly. "And what is that?"

"It deals with the first manifestation you mentioned. You seemed to indicate that core consciousness has a spiritual component to it, and it seems to me that if we are made in God's Image, we must be spiritual beings of some nature. So my question is, how would that spiritual nature be hard-wired into our brains?"

Charlie smiled. "Yeah, I think I wrote you something on that in an email recently. But since we are on the subject, let me ask a different question. What if we do have a spiritual nature and what if that nature is somehow captured in our minds, but not the aspect of mind that emerges from the functionality of the brain? In other words, what if our spiritual nature is somehow reflected in some aspect of mind that manifests elsewhere in the body, or maybe even outside the body?"

"Well, I never expected that to come out of you, Mr. Everything Is A Function Of The Brain, but I guess you are just playing devil's advocate with me."

Charlie winked. "There is always that possibility."

"In which case, I have a very good answer for you. Sure the mind is more than just the brain, but there is no reason some aspect of this spiritual nature—and let's call it the soul right now—could not be reflected in the brain's architecture as well as elsewhere in the body, or outside the body as you suggested."

"OK."

"And so core consciousness and extended consciousness, as you describe them, could easily have contained within them certain basic levels of awareness and capacities for spirituality, could they not? I don't know about you, but I have noticed that some people seem to have no interest, appreciation for, or even psychological inclination toward religious and spiritual matters, while others clearly do. Some people are keenly aware of everything going on around them, or of the needs and concerns of other people, while plenty of other people just live in their own little worlds."

"You are onto something there, Sarah. But I am afraid you have much more understanding than I of core consciousness as it may apply to our spiritual nature, so you will have to fill in some more blanks for me. For example, what exactly do you mean "capacity for spirituality"? How does that manifest, like a capacity for compassion or something like that? And if it is hard-wired, how is it generated? I mean, it seems like the tendency of different people to either be clueless about or sensitive to others' needs is probably a character trait, which could emerge from their core consciousness but also might be entirely learned, perhaps from childhood experiences."

"Aha, now we get to the juicy part—for me anyway, because I love to contemplate my spirituality. First, spirituality for me is defined both by the nature of one's relationship with God and one's capacity for being aware of one's spiritual, or divine, nature. The world of the spirit, whatever that world really constitutes, is different from the physical world, and there are things that can be known and understood in that world and which cannot be explained or apprehended by the logic of the physical world. I suppose you could call the awareness of one's spiritual nature a kind of "spiritual intelligence", which offers a different perspective on the world, a different way of looking at self, or even the meaning of life."

Charlie smiled to himself. He now remembered well the email he had sent Sarah before he left for Boston, in which he had broached the subject, so he wondered if she had developed her thoughts independently or whether his email had indeed invaded her consciousness on the subject. Perhaps it was even a case of memetics at work! It didn't really matter. He was excited about her interest.

"OK, so where does that come from? How do we get such spiritual intelligence into our minds, such that it becomes part of our consciousness, along with all the aspects of consciousness that are always living in the backgrounds of our minds?"

Sarah smiled broadly, savoring the moment. She wanted all of his rapt attention, and her approach seemed to be working. But she hesitated a few moments too long, for suddenly, he threw both his arms around her, and pulled her swiftly to the ground, rolling on top of her in a playful wrestling move, pinning her easily underneath him.

"Tell me, tell me, tell me."

"What's it worth to you?" she managed to giggle.

Charlie lightly forced his weight down on her. "The better question is what is it worth to you for me to let you out of my powerful clutches?"

Sarah called his bluff, now laughing and feigning an attempt at escape. "Oh, heavens, will I be stuck here forever, in the arms of a handsome man, on a beautiful beach in California. What ever will I do?"

He loved it when she laughed like that. It was more than he could resist, and he fell on her half laughing, half crying, kissing her, completely taken up in the moment of deep physical connection, one so satisfying he felt it must be spiritual as well.

chapter 37

It was a day that Charlie knew he would never forget. They decided to leave Crystal Cove and head back to the car, then take the five minute drive down the coast to Laguna Beach and grab some iced coffee drinks, maybe stroll along the boardwalk. During the drive, Charlie returned to their conversation. The nature and depth of the connection he had experienced with Sarah on the beach had made him think again about how she had described spirituality, and that reminded of the fact that there was still something he wanted to learn from her.

"Sarah, you never did tell me about where a person's spiritual consciousness comes from."

"I know, and you never did get done explaining all the five fundamental manifestations of consciousness, but you could excuse a girl for focusing on other things in those circumstances, couldn't you? In fact, I think you could forgive a girl for even forgetting her name in those circumstances. What were they, by the way?"

"What?"

"The other two manifestations of consciousness."

"Oh, that. Well, let's see—we talked about core and extended consciousness, and access consciousness, so that leaves memetically driven consciousness, and finally what I call emergent consciousness. You remember what memes are, right? Well, as the cultures we create to manage human social life generate memes, they begin to have a cumulative effect on what people believe in, the values they exhibit, and what they stand for. For example, your parents implicitly pass many of the environmental influences that affect their thinking on to you, and that thinking, or set of belief systems essentially, slip into your extended experiential consciousness. Moreover, all the memes embedded in those family systems have direct impacts on all of the sub-systems of the social system you live in—you know, like political, economic, legal sub-systems. On top of that, the dynamics of all those systems also directly impact your extended experiential consciousness. For example, I promise you that we have a much different consciousness about the rights, privileges, and dignities of human beings, because of the legal system we live in, than does someone who grew up in Rwanda."

"And finally there is the manifestation I call 'emergent consciousness'. Because through the processes of physical and cultural evolution we humans have developed large, complex brains and intentional minds, we seem to be the only species that is aware of its own self-awareness, or at least the only one with a language that can express that self-awareness. From that self-referential system in our brains, there emerges a special manifestation of consciousness that turns us into moral beings with consciences. I guess you could say conscience is a particular form of human consciousness, which surely must emerge from the many feedback systems within the brain that monitor conditions in the environment, human behavior, and the moral standards of the local culture."

Sarah offered a warm but somewhat sardonic smile. "Whoa, sorry I asked. No really, thanks for the explanation."

Sarah's mind was clearly wandering into some other domain. She was trying to pull herself back into the present but was not succeeding. Charlie didn't press. After a few minutes, she stared straight out into the Pacific, then uttered just three words.

"God does it."

"Does what?"

"Forms our souls, each with its own spiritual character. You wanted to know where our spiritually driven consciousness comes from. God does it. Just like everyone has his or her own personality. Something happens while we are in the womb. It's what Psalm 139 means when it says that God "knits us in our mother's womb". I don't know, maybe it even gets hard-wired into our brains somehow. You would know better than I. Anyway, we all have souls, each with its distinct set of intentionalities and types of consciousness."

Charlie practically ran into the car in front of them. He was so focused on what she was saying, so fascinated by its many implications, he had not even noticed that he had unconsciously raced the speedometer up to 60 and was advancing quickly on the traffic ahead. He decided to pull over to the side of the road. He found a small look-out point and parked. Then he turned off the ignition and turned to her.

"How did you ever come up with that? And what do you mean by 'intentionalities of the soul'?"

"Actually, I have been wrestling with the whole concept of soul for over a year. But you got me to think about what a soul actually is and how it might be registered in the physical body. You know, there are so many people writing about the soul, as if they all knew the answer to something that seems to me unknowable. But it struck me that there must be something to the whole idea of what people want the soul to stand for, or to represent. It must be real—you know, all the stuff that people sense about where they really come from and where they are going, what deep longings live within them while they are alive. I guess that is what I mean by "intentionality of the soul" too—those deep longings we carry around in us. I am not that interested in the metaphysics of the soul—you know, whether it must be attached to a body or not, whether it can reincarnate, etc. etc. So I was looking for a different focus, and when you started talking about how the brain creates the mind, it occurred to me that there might be some similar relationship between the spiritual realm and an individual soul—a phenomenon that emerges from the dynamics of the spiritual world, whatever they might be."

"Oh, are we going to have fun with this one, Sarah. You can teach me so much about spirituality, and I can give you my theories about the nature and source of the mind."

Charlie suddenly stopped short and leaned back, seemingly uneasy with the thought that had just crossed his mind.

"What is it, Charlie?"

"Something I need to ask you about spirituality, but not now. Later, I promise. I just am not ready for it quite yet."

Sarah felt a bit put off, as if Charlie had somehow closed the door on a part of himself and by doing so communicated to her that he was not quite ready for the depth of relationship she yearned for so much. But she knew it would be better to give him the time and space he felt he needed. There would be time enough later, she was sure.

chapter 38

CHARLIE PARKED THE car in the Wild Oats lot and made a note of the time. It would be fine there for an hour. Sarah grabbed her sweater in case they stayed long enough for the late afternoon chill to drift in off the water, and they headed for the boardwalk. When they got to the Pacific Coast Highway, which, in the center of Laguna Beach, usually looked more like a two lane parking lot, Charlie started to turn left toward the Starbucks, but Sarah stopped him.

"Let's go to Dietrichs."

"I like the frappuccinos at Starbucks better."

"Yeah, so do I, but I can't go there any more."

"Why is that?"

"Because my friend Michelle told me that Starbucks is a big supporter of Israel, and Michelle has family in Gaza. Their house has been bulldozed by the Israeli Army just because they wanted to terrorize the community into giving up a suspected Hamas operative. Michelle says that not only does her family know of countless acts of Israeli terrorism against innocent

Palestinians, but that Amnesty International has documented hundreds of other similar incidents, including torture. I will not patronize a company that knowingly supports that sort of state terrorism. Of course, I have a bigger problem now that the U.S. itself seems to be guilty of torture, but I have not worked out yet what to do about that."

Charlie could tell that Sarah was getting increasingly upset. He had not seen that side of her before but respected her point of view. He was not sure about how he felt about the whole situation himself, but it seemed better to just swing by Dietrichs for their coffees.

They lingered for a quite a while on the boardwalk, watching the volleyball players and the kids horsing around on the different types of slides and swings. It had been such a wonderful day, one that had certainly altered the tenor of their relationship, and they decided to sit for a while on the benches facing the ocean, finishing their iced frappuccinos. No deep conversation, just deep satisfaction with the type of relationship that was developing between them. When it was time to go, Charlie rose and pulled Sarah up close to him, kissed her, and locked her arm into his as they strolled along the boardwalk on their way back to the car.

After they crossed Pacific Coast Highway, they waited for the pedestrian signal at the light. Seconds later, it flashed, and they turned to cross. As they started into the street, Sarah tugged affectionately at Charlie's left arm and he turned toward her. It was just a momentary distraction, but it was enough. The driver of the Mercedes had not even really stopped in his hurry to turn right on red and head north on PCH. And for some reason, he did not see Charlie and Sarah as he accelerated into the turn. Charlie's sixth sense alerted him before his eyes did, but it was too late. Charlie instinctively jumped backward, pulling Sarah with him, causing her to tumble, which fortunately accelerated her momentum out of the street on to the sidewalk.

When Charlie felt the impact of the car on his right leg as it trailed behind, he was surprised that the blow did not seem very severe. But the sound of his leg breaking just above the ankle told a different story, and immediately he knew he was trouble. The car slammed to a stop. Sarah screamed. Charlie covered his eyes and waited for the pain.

The thoughts and images that sprinted through his consciousness were of the baseball diamond behind his house in San Diego, and second base specifically. Three years earlier he had sprained the same ankle so badly sliding into second in a pick-up game that he had spent the rest of the summer on crutches. That time, the pain had been excruciating. This time, even though it was the same ankle, it wasn't nearly as bad, but the look in Sarah's eyes told him there was trouble. A crowd started to gather, and finally, reluctantly, Charlie sat up and turned toward his leg to assess the damage. Sarah stopped him.

"Charlie, don't. Don't move. I think your leg is broken, so don't try to get up or anything. Oh damn, why couldn't it have been me? Just stay still. I'll get help."

Sarah rushed past the driver of the Mercedes, who was standing by helplessly, aware that there had been plenty of witnesses and wondering how he was going to explain his carelessness. Sarah spotted a policeman and asked him to call the paramedics, and he nodded affirmatively. The Laguna Beach Fire Department was only about eight blocks away, and she knew they would be there shortly. A lifeguard had made his way over as well, and he tried to disperse the crowd a little. Charlie did not even try to turn himself over and sit up. Blood was already tricking down his leg, where the compound fracture had cut through the surface flesh.

The paramedics were predictably professional, but even they could not disguise their dismay at how bad the break was. If they had known Charlie was an athlete who was already familiar with the many things that can go wrong in one's body, they might have been less concerned about how they answered Charlie's first question.

"How bad is it, guys?"

"Looks like a compound fracture, but they will fix you up just fine at the hospital. We will be at Saddleback in 15 minutes. How is your pain?"

"Not too bad, really, but I can't feel my right foot right now."

One of the paramedics shot the other one a quick glance. "Well, we gave you a little something to ease the pain, so it's probably kicked in already."

Charlie wasn't convinced. He looked at Sarah for help. She was fighting back tears. He forgot his own fears and focused on her.

"Hey, Sarah, now you will be the one visiting *me* at Saddleback. Weird, huh?"

Sarah was not in the least bit surprised that Charlie was trying to take it all in stride, trying to distract her. It was one of the reasons she had fallen so deeply in love with him. He had a certain way about him, a self-bearing that made it clear he could handle crises with courage and dignity, that he could cope with dangerous situations, that he could always keep his wits about him. She wanted to collect herself and let him know he could quit concerning himself with how *she* was feeling.

"Yeah, I guess it will be a little strange, going back there so soon. But at least you won't be there as long as I was. Heck, they will probably plaster you up and throw you out tomorrow."

"Let's hope so. The draft is next week, and I want to be able to go to Boston after I get selected."

Sarah summoned all of her limited acting skills and managed to force a smile, because her heart was sinking. She had not thought about the draft, but obviously that was the first thing that had crossed Charlie's mind. Now she wondered whether he was an incurable optimist or just incredibly naïve, because as little as she knew about baseball and the draft, she instinctively found it hard to believe that his injury would not affect his perceived value, and therefore his draft position.

"Right. And I am sure you will be taking me with you, right Charlie?"

It was a little devious, especially under the circumstances, but the ploy was a good one, immediately shifting Charlie's consciousness away from the draft and onto his feelings about Sarah. He had not thought about whether he would be inviting Sarah to go with him to his agent's office during draft day. For the most part, he had not thought about the logistics at all, relying mostly on the anecdotal accounts of the process he had picked up from Neal and a few of his teammates who seemed to know more about the whole process. But the question did make him focus on Sarah and his relationship with her.

"Why not? That sounds like a great idea. Maybe your mom would want to come too."

Sarah studied his face, to make sure there was no trace of sarcasm. No, not Charlie. That wasn't his style.

"Oh, I am sure she would! But I am not so sure I am willing to share you with both the Red Sox and her!"

Charlie smiled. There certainly could be no doubt knowing Sarah Wilson's intentions when she wanted them to be well understood.

chapter 39

THE ORTHOPEDIC SURGEON confirmed the paramedics' initial diagnosis. The impact had snapped both the tibia and the fibia of Charlie's right leg, and the doctor had had to put plates in both to set them properly. He promised Charlie a full and complete recovery, but he obviously could not assure him that the break would not affect his ability to play baseball at the highest levels. No doubt the Red Sox orthopedic expert would have an opinion that would be far more relevant anyway.

Sarah had been right—Charlie was discharged from the hospital the next day, and she drove him back to her apartment so she could look after him. She had decided she could simply ferry him back to his dorm room in the evening and get him again in the morning, at least for a few days. He probably would get tired of being tended to that closely after that. She had thought of the possibility of inviting him to stay with her, all under the guise of making sure he was OK and getting whatever he needed, but decided it might seem a bit forward. Sarah thought Charlie was the kind of guy who wanted to call those shots and might be turned off by a woman who was too suggestive or pushy. As they drove north on the 405, Charlie seemed to have slipped into an uncharacteristically somber mood.

"Sarah, do you believe in fate?"

"Where did that one come from? And what do you mean by 'fate'?"

"Oh, I was just thinking. About my leg and all. And the draft. What if the Red Sox get spooked and drop me down the draft chart, or off it? What if I don't get drafted at all? I mean that would certainly change my future. I could still try out with some other team, of course, but my odds of making it would certainly go down. And what if that is just the way it is supposed to be? What if it just is not part of my fate to be a major league player."

"Well, in the first place, you are right, you don't even know now what will happen. You might end up being drafted by another team and land with them, where you might not have with the Sox, just because of who else they have on their roster. So it is way too early to think about not playing baseball. But since you brought it up, no, I don't believe in fate the way I think you, and most other people, mean it. And I certainly don't believe in any kind of divine predestination for our lives either. However, I do think God has certain hopes, perhaps even something akin to expectations, for our lives. I know it sounds a bit anthropomorphic to speak of God that way, but I do think that somehow there are certain expectations for what we might do in life. God wants us to learn how to overcome our natural inclination to think about ourselves first, so that we eventually become primarily oriented toward the other. And I believe there are ways that God works, all quite mysterious to us when we try to understand them logically and linearly, to encourage and perhaps facilitate some of what we end up doing and standing for in our lives. But ultimately, I believe in free will, because I think God set in motion a fabulously complex and beautiful process for Creation and that it is up to us what we choose to do with all of that bounty."

Charlie sighed, seemingly uneasy. "But Sarah, does that mean we have specific things we are meant to do in life? Does our free will not only empower us but demand that we figure out exactly what we are supposed to do in life?"

"No, I don't think so, but maybe I should make an important distinction here. To the extent that I claimed God 'cares' about anything, I think that applies more generally to all humanity. So I would say God cares that eventually we begin to make better choices, as a species, and start to evolve toward becoming truly other oriented beings. On the other hand, I could see where Jesus, who is sort of a different manifestation of God, might actually 'care' about who we are as individuals and how we behave toward each other, today. The great thing about Jesus is that he not only revealed a little bit of what God is like but demonstrated for us what humans are actually capable of—in fact, the famous French philosopher, Pierre Teilhard de Chardin, even described us not as *human* beings who have spiritual experiences but as spiritual beings who are having a human experience. So Jesus showed us what it would look like to be a truly evolved spiritual being having a human experience, and in doing so, I suppose he also demonstrated that he 'cares' that we all aspire to that."

"So what I hear you saying is that maybe God does not care whether we do good things in careers as baseball players or doctors or teachers or writers but does care that we learn important lessons and begin to orient ourselves more toward others, and at the same time Jesus might 'care' how we go about doing that, regardless of what our professions are. Is that right?"

"Yeah, that's right. And so in that context 'fate' doesn't really compute, because regardless of what happens to you and what paths you choose to take in life, what is really at stake is whether you are becoming less oriented toward your own desires and more focused on the needs of others."

"And what about our meeting, where does that fit into the scheme of things according to that thinking?"

"You mean were we somehow 'fated', or designed to meet, so we would somehow each be better enabled to choose well and become more other oriented?"

"Precisely."

"I figured you might be going there. I don't have a good answer for you on that one. When I was a girl, I always thought that there was one man for me, out there somewhere in the world, and all I had to do was go find him. I suppose it was a concept like the one people generally refer to as 'soul mate'. But I used to talk with my mother a lot about that idea, and she has pretty much convinced me that even if there were such a phenomenon as a soul mate who is somehow connected in spirit, there would be many such people, not just one, and they could vary in degree of importance in your life."

"That's a compelling position, Sarah, but you didn't really answer my question."

"I know. I should have known better than to think you wouldn't notice."

"And so?"

"And so, in case you have not figured it out by now, Charlie Howell, I am very much in love with you and feel deeply spiritually connected to you as well, but I don't think you are my one and only soul mate, whom I was destined to meet, so that my life could be defined by you and our relationship to each other. How is that, clear enough for you?"

Charlie was intrigued by the tone of Sarah's voice. It seemed so assured, as if she had not a doubt in her mind that she would spend the rest of her life with him, even as she was explaining that she didn't think they were somehow destined to be together. Nor was he particularly startled to hear her express her love for him so easily and confidently. He was surely not as comfortable doing so, but he found her conviction neither surprising nor the source of any artificial pressure. He sensed he would get there in his own time. He was more interested in something else she said. It reminded him of the subject he had wanted to discuss with her at the beach but had not felt quite ready to take on. He wondered if that was the way it worked in God's world too, that you kept receiving intimations of thoughts or actions you would eventually undertake at some later date, when some other set of circumstances brought the opportunity into full focus.

"Sarah, remember yesterday when I said there was something I wanted to ask you but wasn't quite ready?"

"Yeah."

"Well, I didn't expect it to happen this soon, but it came back to me as you were talking and now I am ready."

Sarah felt a little butterfly flutter in her stomach, a butterfly of anticipation, but of the delightful variety. She could not think of anything that they had talked about in the last two days that she would not like to dig into more deeply, especially if in doing so Charlie revealed more of his feelings.

"And I am all ears."

"Actually, that's a very silly expression, since all our 'listening' really takes place in a certain region of the brain, and it's more important to get your consciousness and working memory focused on what is being said than it is…"

Sarah was giving him a playfully annoyed look, or maybe it wasn't that playful after all.

"Right, never mind. Back to my question. Do you remember when you were talking about your notion that maybe God hard-wires our brains for spiritual consciousness or imbues us with some sort of spiritual intelligence?"

"Yes."

"Well, do you think possibly that our brains could be wired in such a way that the physical and emotional affection that we feel for other people is connected to the spiritual connection we have with God?"

Sarah didn't answer right away. Slowly, she guided the car over toward the right hand lane and eventually onto the shoulder of the highway. When the car had stopped, she turned to him, smiling through a stream of tears.

"Oh, Charlie, I do believe that. How did you know? Yes, I believe with all my heart that what we can come to experience in physical and emotion intimacy with each other is indeed a *representation* of the love that God has for us. I believe that emotional intimacy is one of God's greatest gifts to humanity."

Tears began to form in Charlie's eyes as well. He was not exactly sure why. He couldn't associate it with any feeling he was familiar with, though he was certainly sensing lots of emotion coursing through his mind and body. More than anything, he just sensed the overwhelming intimacy between them, so he reached around her neck and pulled her to him, kissing her passionately, as tears continue to stream down both their faces.

When they released their embrace and sat back in their seats, Sarah spoke first.

"Let's get off this highway and find some place we can talk."

Culver Drive was just a mile ahead, so Sarah exited the 405 and turned left, toward the UCI campus. Then she made a left on Michelson and turned into the shopping center on the corner of Michelson and Culver, where her favorite coffee shop, Café City, was located.

Soon they were enjoying their lattes on a bench outside the shop.

"You know, Charlie, it is so interesting that you framed that concept in terms of the wiring in our brains. I have been thinking about that idea for a couple of years now, trying to reconcile my own deep physical urgings with my sense of spirituality and my developing love for God. And yesterday was the first time I thought about grounding my feelings in any place in my body, or mind. I certainly had not thought about the brain. But you, Mr. Brainiac, you have this fantastic vision of the mind and how it emerges from the wiring of our brains. You really are an amazing man, and there is so much more I want to learn from you."

"So what exactly do you think the connection is, Sarah? I mean, how does emotional love and intimacy apply to both our relationships with each other and to our relationships with God? And why do we translate that into physical sensations and feelings in our love relationships with each other, though obviously that element is missing in our relationships with God?"

"Well, first of all, I am not sure it is missing from our relationships with God. I have had a few experiences in church when I felt God's immediate presence, and there were definite physical aspects to that experience. Could I call the experience of that presence love, or relate it to intimacy with a man? I don't know, but my sense is that there is something that both those phenomena share in common. What I think about most is how I *feel* when I am sensing a proximity to God, and how I *feel* when I sense a deep intimacy with another person."

Charlie knew there was a logical question to follow on what Sarah had just said but had no idea how to ask it. So he decided just to toss it out there in front of them, unvarnished and unavoidable.

"What about sex, how does that come into it?"

To her credit, Sarah was neither unprepared to answer the question nor seemingly uncomfortable with doing so.

"Yes, the complicated issue of sex. If we were just talking about spirituality, I would say unequivocally that sexual intimacy is the great connection we have between our physical and spiritual selves. We have divinity within us, so we know how to express and experience the love of God. But to experience our divinity, we must also know its antithesis, our humanity. I think that in loving another deeply we get in touch with the divine in us, and when we consummate that love in an act of sexual intimacy, we merge our experience of the divine with our physical humanity. And then there is a sharing element to it as well. Sexual intimacy occurs when each lover finds that the other not only wants to give of him or herself to the other but is enjoying doing so."

Charlie was starting to blush, but Sarah continued, seemingly perfectly comfortable in the conversation. "Unfortunately, religious beliefs have complicated this view, attempting to prescribe when sexual intimacy between two people is considered "right" or "Godly", perhaps in the attempt to legislate what is thought to be a set of desirable family values, like monogamy, or perhaps to maintain some moral authority. Certainly, there is no question that sex is a very complex sociological phenomenon, and inevitably religions like to stake their positions on such phenomena. The question I always ask myself when it comes to matters of sexual intimacy is "what is God more interested in, the full and creative expression of love or a set of rules and social conventions?"

Charlie decided that as long as he had opened Pandora's Box, he might as well investigate all its contents.

"But what have you *experienced,* Sarah? I mean, independent of the moral or religious principles involved?"

Sarah finally appeared a little uncomfortable, but her passion for the subject sustained her commitment to the conversation.

"That's sort of the point, Charlie. I can't help but be influenced by my religious convictions, which frankly do cause me some confusion in the matter. But I guess I would say that if two people love each other, sexual intimacy is a great gift to be enjoyed, without regard to whether they are married and without regard to their sexual orientation. The only proviso I would add is that the gift must be enjoyed responsibly—if engaging in sexual intimacy hurts someone else, as for example, in the case of marital infidelity, then that's a different story."

Charlie suddenly felt like he had seen more of Pandora's Box than he wanted. There needed to be a little mystery in his developing relationship with Sarah, especially on the physical side. Exploration was part of the enjoyment, and he didn't want to know all of

Sarah's thoughts about sexual intimacy. He decided to change the subject.

"Sarah, can we talk about something else?"

"Sure. Why? Does talking about sex make you uncomfortable?"

"I suppose in a way, yes."

"All right. What do you want to talk about?"

"Your feelings for me. Are you really in love with me?"

"Maybe not such a great shift in topic after all. Yes, I am really in love with you. Until yesterday, I would have said that I loved you. Today, I know I am *in love* with you. There's a difference you know."

Charlie was once again impressed by Sarah's forthrightness, but the strength of her feelings surprised him. She seemed so facile with talking about herself and her feelings.

"What do you think the difference is?"

"I think it's similar to the difference between sympathy and compassion."

Charlie looked confused. "Go on."

"Yeah, while sympathy involves extending one's concern toward another, compassion requires an entering into the life of the other. The emphasis is being "with" the other. So, loving someone can result from respecting him deeply, appreciating aspects of his character, and other such connections, but being in love, well, that's more like being part of the other, having entered into the heart and mind of the other. When you are in love with someone, as I am with you, you are willing to sacrifice much more of what you want for the mutual benefit of both. I know I don't want to lose myself in our relationship but I want to be a part of you, for sure."

Sarah stopped, suddenly mindful of the fact that though all this was very clear to her, having rehearsed it thousands of times over the last few years, it might seem a bit intimidating to someone else. Fortunately, Charlie did not seem uneasy.

"That's so cool, Sarah. And the more you talk, the more I continue to fall in love with you too. How did you ever get to be so wise about all this stuff?"

"Probably the same way you became such an expert on the brain. It just comes out of me, and I am always interested in learning more. I suppose it's just something that I am passionate about. Maybe it's just knowledge that is embedded in my soul, part of what you would call my core consciousness I suppose."

"Yeah, I certainly can relate to that."

chapter 40

CHARLIE'S FIRST ORDER of business was to call Jim Rogers, his agent in Newport Beach. Jim had relocated to California from the Philadelphia area, where he had spent most of his life, both before and after graduating from Rutgers Law School. He had played baseball at Princeton and tried out with the Mets and Rangers, but he had quickly come to the realization that his future in baseball should be as an agent, not a player. He had joined Leigh Steinberg in Newport Beach two years after graduation from Rutgers and had been successfully filling the Steinberg stable with rising major league stars for the past 10 years. Charlie thought he was lucky to have him as an agent and was grateful to the UCI booster who had made the introduction for him.

Unfortunately, today's conversation was not going to be one either of them would enjoy. Charlie got through immediately.

"Jim Rogers."

"Jim, it's Charlie Howell. How are you doing?"

"Fine, Charlie. Fine. How are you? Staying in fighting shape I trust?"

"Unfortunately, Jim, that's why I am calling. I had an accident. Compound fracture of my right leg."

"You're kidding. Tell me you're kidding. The draft is next week. What the hell happened?"

Charlie felt some mild irritation building. "Don't you think I know the draft is next week, Jim? It's not like I planned this or did something stupid like go skiing!"

"Charlie, I'm sorry. I didn't mean it like that. I am just shocked. Sorry. What did happen? I will have to call Neal, you know, and let them know."

"Of course. That's why I called you. I trust it won't be a big deal. I got hit by a car while crossing PCH in Laguna Beach. It was a double compound fracture, but the doc said everything will be fine."

"I hate to say this, Charlie, but it could be a problem. You don't know these guys like I do. They're pretty skittish about injuries."

"Really? Even broken legs? It's not like I blew out a knee."

"Yes, even broken legs, but especially with compound fractures. Sorry, but I know you always want me to be straight with you. Listen, I will call them today and get back to you. I don't want to keep you on pins and needles."

"Thanks, Jim. I appreciate that."

"Sure. By the way, was it your fault? We might want to think about getting lawyers involved."

"No, definitely not my fault. I was crossing PCH, on the light. Some guy in a hurry didn't stop to look when he turned right on red. His Mercedes caught me just as I looked back and saw him."

The word "Mercedes" touched off another set of neurons in Jim's brain. At least Charlie would be well compensated if his draft position slipped.

"Well, the Sox do seem to love you, so I hope this blows over. If not, somebody's going to pay."

Spoken like a true agent/lawyer, Charlie thought to himself. "I am counting on you, Jim."

"I will see what I can do, Charlie."

chapter 41

CHARLIE WAS SITTING on the couch in Sarah's apartment, his broken leg propped up, feeling anxious about the draft. Jim had called back with just a brief message that the Sox were upset with the news but had communicated little else. Charlie needed something else to focus on, and Sarah was happy to keep him company.

"Sarah, you're the expert on this. Let me ask you, why is religion the cause of so many problems in the world, when religious morals would seem to dictate just the opposite?"

"What kind of morals are you thinking about? Some religious morals can be easily misguided and misapplied, causing great harm."

"I was thinking particularly of the Golden Rule—don't do to others what you would not like done to you, or do unto others what you would have done to you. My understanding is that this moral imperative is common to all the world's major religions, and those are the ones I am concerned with, not some fringe group of religious fanatics."

"Yes, I think that's right, and my answer is going to be right up your alley."

"Really?"

"Really. You see, from my point of view the main problem with religion is that it has become a social phenomenon, *cognitively* developed from the outset to help individuals deal with some difficult metaphysical questions but later hijacked by various powerful people trying to promote their own interests or social agendas. You are seeing it all over the place in American society today, where religion may have moved closer to being a pure sociological phenomenon, and farther away from a belief system that promotes spiritual journey, than at any other time in modern western history. I think that institutionalized religion has even become western so-ciety's biggest purveyor of *memes!*"

"I am impressed, Sarah. Apparently, you like the concept of memes."

"Indeed I do, and I have thought a lot about memes since you brought it up the other day."

"Great, but let's go back a step. When you refer to religion as being 'cognitive', you mean it has become ra-tionally calculating, geared to achieving certain ends?"

"Yes, that's a good way of putting it, Charlie, but I also want to convey the idea that religion has become too much of a matter of the 'head' rather than the 'heart'. We want to *think* about everything and make sense of it, rather than accepting that God, and the do-main of the Spirit, can never really be fully understood. Religion should be the domain of spiritual journey, where we simply encounter life, then learn and grow spiritually from our experiences of it."

"I see. OK, so back to my question—why has religion wrought such terrible division and hatred over the years? What can't religious people follow the morality of the Golden Rule?"

"Right. You should like this. I believe that because of the way our brains work, we are inherently fearful, self-centered people. It's just a fact of life. We take care of ourselves first, then invoke the social exigency and morality of tending to others, not vice versa. We are wired to think first of what we want to eat today before we can think about whether others will be eating at all. So while the Golden Rule makes sense as a set of *memes* that help maintain order in society and different religious institutions, it is actually a very difficult thing for humans to practice. Mind you, as you have pointed out yourself, the brain is a social organ as well, so it is also wired to seek out the other and build community, even act altruistically, but unfortunately, that's where the fear part kicks in. Very often, when we build our communities, we start to think that the security of our belonging will eradicate all our fears, but it does not. We just learn to fear different things. That is precisely what happens with religious practice and communities—we think we are going to act differently when we belong to religious communities, but for the most part, we don't."

"So, Sarah, what you are saying is that even in religious communities we end up acting fearfully, excluding others whom we don't think belong in *our* community. Then of course, once we start excluding people, the morality of the Golden Rule goes right out the window."

"Exactly."

"And how do we avoid that trap, in our religious communities or elsewhere?"

"Well, for one, overcoming our fears. So often religious leaders play on our fears and get us to think things that might enhance their power and authority but don't do much to transform our fears. The practice of religion ought to involve the journey into our spiritual nature, and the expression of that spiritual nature is what will banish our fears."

"How exactly?"

"We learn to trust in the abundance of God's Creation. We learn to let go of our compulsion to plan and control everything. We learn to love others and have faith that in kind we will be treated with love. Love is so powerful because it regenerates itself—the more love you express, the more you have available to keep sharing, and eventually the love you share becomes the love you experience for yourself. Loving others necessarily takes us outside ourselves, forces us to consider other points of view, and disrupts our closed systems of belief."

Charlie was beginning to pick up the scent. "Which is critical to our being able to actually apply the Golden Rule, right? I mean, to practice the morality of the Golden Rule, it seems that we must engage in a certain amount of translation, right? For example, if I said I like people to be responsive to me, I ought to be responsive to others in return, in which case I first need to understand what it is that they seek."

Sarah thought for a minute. "Yes, that is a good point, but we can use our own experiences in the process of discovering what other people seek or need. For example, I believe we are called to examine our own illusions, pain, and sadness, so that we can help others deal with theirs, or perhaps even avoid some of the pain that has visited us."

"How did you get so smart about these things, Sarah?"

Sarah blushed. Actually, she wasn't sure how to answer that question, because she really didn't know how these ideas came so readily to her. She decided on a compromise. "It's not too complicated. I just focus on trying to be aware, aware of what life is about, what's going on around me, what other people are thinking, that sort of thing."

"But doesn't that make you vulnerable to a lot of heartache, your own and that of others you become aware of?"

"Yes, I suppose it does. I guess that is the price one pays for becoming aware, for waking up to what life means and what is really going on for millions of other people. We don't do a great job of that in this country. Most Americans are pretty insular, or perhaps they are just unwilling to deal with the pain that comes from being aware of how difficult life is for so many people in this world. I am always amazed at how many Americans have no idea how good they have it compared to most other people in the world. As you would say, we prefer that our 'access consciousness' is focused on ourselves, our families, and perhaps our communities, rather than the whole world. Maybe we are just afraid of being overwhelmed by life's miseries, because we have had two generations now of Americans who have known very little hardship."

"Sounds a little depressing."

Sarah gave him a wry smile. She couldn't resist. "Just depends on your consciousness, Charlie."

chapter 42

TWO DAYS BEFORE the draft Charlie woke up with an uncomfortable feeling. His leg was hurting him a little, but that was not as troubling as the sensation he carried that this was not going to be a great day.

Sarah called to say she was coming over and bringing breakfast. Charlie knew that would help his mood, but part of him wanted to be alone, to deal with whatever disappointment loomed on the horizon. Sure enough, just before she arrived, the Red Sox called.

"Charlie, this is Bob Neal. How are you doing? I was really shocked to hear about your leg. I am so sorry."

"Thanks, Bob. Pretty lousy timing, huh? But I will be OK. Don't you guys worry about it. In three months, I will be good as new."

"I hope so, Charlie. I really do. Listen, Charlie, I wanted to call before the draft, so you weren't blindsided by anything. You are a stand-up kind of guy and you deserve to know what's going on."

Charlie felt a rush of blood surge into his chest and neck. He knew what was coming.

Neal continued. "Charlie, we have to pass on you. Not just on the second round, the whole draft. We just felt we couldn't take a chance on your recovery. I know it sounds like chicken shit, and I don't blame you for thinking we are idiots, but I wanted you to know what we decided. We had too many guys we are keen on to take a chance on your leg. For what it's worth, I didn't agree with the decision, but I was overruled, and then of course I was given the assignment to inform you. It took me a day to gin up the emotional energy, and right now I feel sick to my stomach. But I guess that does not change anything about the way you feel. I am really, really sorry, Charlie."

Charlie suddenly realized that he felt quite calm. "I figured that was why you were calling. And I won't lie to you, it is a blow. I had some strangely foreboding sensations this morning, but I still could not make myself believe that it would happen. But thank you for your personal sentiments, Bob. It actually means a lot to me."

"Thanks. And Charlie, the reason I didn't agree with the decision is I still believe you will play, so don't give up just because of what we did as an organization. That's what organizations do, you know, they take the path of least resistance and lowest risk. But I think I know the kind of person you are, and if anyone can do it, you can. Success in life has much more to do with who you are and the nature of your character than the talent you are born with. I know you understand that, and I know you will succeed whatever you end up doing."

"If you don't mind, I want to give you one more piece of advice on that front. As you would well appreciate, I am convinced that the human brain is built to turn conscious learning into unconscious knowledge and that successful people use that to their advantage. They generate unconscious habits and strategies that continue to feed their expertise, self-control, and motivation. I have no doubt that you will do the same, and I look forward to following your career, wherever it takes you, so I hope will stay in touch. And if there is any way I can help, you just let me know. Successful people invariably are helped along by good mentors too, and if I can serve as such for you, I would be honored. You still have my cell number?"

"Yes. Thanks, Bob. I really appreciate the offer, and I will take you up on it when the time comes. "

"Good luck with your rehab, Charlie. I will call Jim and tell him as well, of course, in case he wants to make some quick calls to other clubs."

"OK, thanks."

"Bye."

"Bye."

Charlie hung up just as he heard Sarah's knock. As he moved toward the door, he felt a new sensation. At first, he was not even sure what it was, a wave of emotion perhaps, maybe some deep seated memory that had been triggered by the conversation with Bob Neal, which had all the ingredients of a personal rejection, even though it seemed a perfectly rational decision in many respects. Something had touched a nerve.

Charlie opened the door and Sarah practically leapt into this arms, pulling back just in time, remembering his leg.

"Hi, sailor. Looking for a good time?"

Charlie wanted to respond with equal cheer but just could not. "Not today, unfortunately. The Red Sox just called. They aren't taking me in the draft."

Sarah's face fell, but she rallied. "I'm so sorry, Charlie. That is so stupid. Just because of your leg?"

"Yes, they said they couldn't take a chance I might not be ready next year."

"So you can just call some other clubs, right? What about the Cubs, weren't they interested?"

"I don't know. I need some time to deal with this. I am sure Jim will look into the other options." Charlie suddenly felt really down. There was definitely something else going on, deep in his soul.

"Hey, Charlie, you never know. It might work out for the best. Maybe a team that is not as deep in shortstops as the Sox will be even more interested than they were. Look on the plus side."

Charlie didn't feel like being positive and didn't think there was much chance that something better could come of the Sox's decision. He had become emotionally attached to the idea of being a member of the Red Sox, and it hurt to know that was not going to happen.

"Sarah, can we forget breakfast and take a walk?"

Sarah looked at him quizzically. This was a side of Charlie she had never seen. He seemed distracted, almost lost, and surely she had never seen him without an appetite. "Sure, Charlie, whatever you want."

Charlie helped her put the food away, then grabbed her hand and headed for the door. He needed fresh air. Something dark was crowding in on him.

chapter 43

THEY HAD BEEN sitting for over 15 minutes, and Charlie had barely said a word. He had tired quickly during their walk, still laboring a bit on his crutches, and decided to sit down on the grass rather than return to the apartment.

"Charlie, what's wrong? I have never seen you like this."

Tears started to form in his eyes. He didn't try to stop them. "When I was a kid, I remember having only two dreams. One was to play baseball with my dad, but he died before we ever got a chance. The other was to play in the majors. I feel like that one died today."

"Oh, sweetie, no. It's not over. Not by a long shot. Even if you don't get drafted, I know you. You will rehab harder than anyone ever has, be in better shape than the rest of the rookies, and probably march right into the Red Sox camp, without having been drafted, and win a job."

"Yeah, maybe."

Sarah grabbed his left arm and turned him towards her, rather forcefully. "OK, buddy what *really* gives?"

Her demeanor startled him, and he hesitated. He took a deep breath and gave a long, low sigh.

"When I was about fifteen, I got really sad, just missing my dad so much, and Mom sent me to see a counselor at school. We talked a lot about my dad and my feelings, and she ended up recommending that I read a book by John Eldredge entitled *Wild at Heart*. It's about the woundedness that every man suffers if he does not have a dad around—for whatever reason—to help him gain the confidence that he has what it takes to make it in the world. According to Eldredge, one of the key roles of a father is to provide calculated challenges to his sons, based on their aptitudes and ambitions, so that they learn, by trial, error, and eventual success, that they have what it takes to survive in a competitive male environment. Eldredge says that if you don't get that from your father at an early age, you spend the rest of your life either trying to prove to yourself and others that you have what it takes, or you struggle so much with self doubt that you never fully embrace the 'wild', untamed, adventurous part of your heart and forever carry the wound of not having fully experienced yourself. My counselor thought that much of my sadness was not so much missing my dad as not having discovered my 'wild heart'. She said that did not mean I had to go become a rebel teenager but that I would have to find my 'wild heart' all by myself, that I would have to start viewing life differently, with a greater sense of mystery. She said that I should not be afraid of embracing adventure, but it always seemed to me that I did not need to go looking for any particular kind of adventure, because baseball and the mysteries of science presented more than enough of the unknown for me. This morning all that came rushing back to me, and it occurred to me that maybe the time had come for me to start pursuing my 'wild heart' and new adventures, to let go of baseball and open up my world a little. But in the process, all that old emotion about missing my dad just welled up in my being and has made me feel really sad. That, and I am not ready to quit baseball."

Sarah held him close for some time. "Then don't quit, honey. And as far as your dad is concerned, just let the sadness come on. It's there, and just like we were talking earlier, you just have to let those things flow. Sometimes it's time to let them flow so you can let go of them. Sometimes they just need to flow out to release the pressure, because they are never going to go away completely. You will always miss your dad—you just can't let it eat at you, so just let the sadness flow. I am right here."

"Thanks, Sarah. I feel better already."

"Take your time, Charlie. And as to the other thing about your 'wild heart', there might be something to that too. Being female, I obviously cannot fully appreciate the male psyche or the phenomenon you are talking about, but I wouldn't rush into anything. Take your time with that too. Heck, draft day isn't even over, so you don't even know that another club isn't dying to have you."

"Intellectually, I know all that is true, but there is something deep within me that seems to connect with a wound that has no rational dimension to it. The crazy thing is I almost feel like there is this sensation of joy trying to emerge—you know, like the sun as it peeks through a thick mist. But I also feel pretty raw, so be gentle with me, Sarah. You don't need to even really understand it, but please be gentle."

"I know, Charlie. I will." Making sure not to lay on his right leg, she snuggled up to him and gave him a lasting kiss. She hoped it would convey every bit of the compassion and love she was feeling. She had never felt such deep respect and affection for a man before, and she wanted him to know it. Whatever it was that lived in a man's heart when he experienced an existential doubt about what he was doing in the world and why, Sarah figured it must be a lonely journey, and if Charlie Howell needed her in any way, she was going to be there for him.

chapter 44

WHEN THEY GOT back to the apartment, Charlie checked his cell phone for messages. There was one from Jim Rogers saying that he had contacted the Cubs and the Braves, the other clubs that had called over the last two weeks to talk about their interests in Charlie, but neither one would make any promises. Jim tried to reassure Charlie that something might still happen and that he should just relax and take care of his leg. Charlie knew it was all code for "sorry, but your leg break spooked everyone" and that he didn't need to worry about keeping his cell phone close by for the rest of the day. There wouldn't be any calls, especially not from Jim, who would be busy with other players. Sarah seemed temporarily distracted by a need to clean up her kitchen, so Charlie grabbed his journal and plunked himself down on the couch.

"I am wondering whether the way into this wound—this existential doubt about whether if I were never to play baseball again I could find my way in the world—is

through consciousness. Sarah keeps pointing out how we are spiritual beings, which must mean we have some aspect to the self that can transcend the limits of our physical nature, perhaps even the limits of our known brain functions, and if that is true, I must have within me some ability to go beyond the limitations of my current thoughts and feelings. Certainly it is true that the brain itself is highly plastic and can even restructure itself, growing new neurons as well as reconfiguring existing ones, all of which suggests that my mind, my thoughts, and my feelings can undergo significant change if I choose to make that happen. But can I produce that through the exercise of sheer will? Can I choose to become other than what I seem to be, based on the accumulation of my experiences so far in life? I know there is recent research that suggests we can consciously choose to forget certain types of memories and eradicate some of the negative feelings associated with them. So it seems to me that it must be theoretically possible to change anything we want about ourselves, our thoughts, even our moods, especially if our minds are indeed emergent phenomena that can exert causal influences on the brain structure from which it emerges.

Maybe the place to start is to distinguish between the autobiographical self that is an emergent property of the brain and the self that generates our deepest desires, our most cherished visions. If I look at it in that framework, it seems to make sense that I could choose a different trajectory for my autobiographical self. Why shouldn't I be able to choose a new "destiny", perhaps even to the point of living into a spiritual reality that by design has been left open for me to embrace when the time is right? Sure, to some extent my brain was hard wired a certain way from birth, in order to give me certain aspects of personality, perhaps specific talents and intelligence, but if I can expand those capacities by working my brain harder, if I can become more intelligent or learn a new language, why couldn't I also "expand" the nature of my autobiographical self, since it too is simply a function of brain mechanics?

A thought suddenly struck him. "Hey, Sarah, come here a minute", he exclaimed excitedly. She was by his side in a flash, intrigued by Charlie's enthusiasm and change of mood.

"What is it?"

"I was just journaling some things, following on our conversation this morning, and something in particular struck me. Remember when we were talking about the relationship between spirituality and sexuality, and you said that you thought God might imbue each of us with our own unique expressions of the divine, in the form of a soul, or I suppose a 'spiritual DNA'?"

"Yeah, why?"

"Well, lots of neuroscientists have been so consumed with the whole matter of consciousness, and surely it is a critical driver of human behavior. But suppose that the really important elements of human nature, such as awareness of God, ability to love unconditionally, or capacity for compassion, are not so much emergent properties of the brain's self-organizing adaptive system as they are products of an interactive *relationship* between the human body's neurological systems and some aspect of God's Spirit—at a quantum, or even sub-quantum level. In other words, maybe a core element of human consciousness is rooted in the dynamic interaction between the 'information' encoded in the brain that reflects a person's 'spiritual DNA' and the divine intelligence we talked about earlier? You know, sort of in the same way that information encoded in your DNA forms your body and directs its functioning. In other words, just as the information in your genes reflects millions of years of evolution, which gets expressed in your own unique phenotype, the divine intelligence that lies behind the self-organization of our universe gets expressed in the 'spiritual genes' of your soul."

Sarah could tell Charlie was really charged up and ready to go on, but she wasn't. She wanted to slow the whole process down. "Be more specific, Charlie. How would that work exactly?"

"Well, Sarah, I am still working that out, but how about this? Think about what we have called 'spiritual DNA' as a *matrix* of information in the sense that all energy is information and could therefore be embedded not only in the brain's neurons but all cells in the body, say, at a quantum level. There are issues about whether information could be held in quantum superposition within living cells, since there is the problem of decoherence, but let's leave that aside for the moment. After all, I am just thinking out loud at this point. Anyway, that matrix could have different forms of information in it, some of which would relate to the makeup of the person's soul—the spiritual DNA—some of which would carry the collective consciousness of the entire human species, and some of which would provide the translation software that allows the brain to tap into the universe's self-organizing, adaptive intelligence—you know, sort of like operating software in a computer."

"That's pretty wild, Mr. Charlie Howell. Did you get a little too much Darvon in your system this morning? Or maybe you just wanted to go ahead and find that— what was it—'wild heart' right away, huh?"

"No, I am dead serious, and I would have thought that you, of all people, would be ecstatic."

"Of course I am Charlie. I was just trying to lighten things up a bit. You may or may not remember that 15 minutes ago you were in a pretty down mood. Besides, this is all a little heady for me. I don't know the first thing about quantum mechanics, for example."

"Yeah, you're right. I have been a bit over the top lately. I am sure that is something I still need to dig into. Don't you think it's fun to play with theories, though?"

"Oh, sure, and any theory of yours is of interest to me. Just remember that it's not always easy for a poor little music major like me to keep up."

"Yeah, poor little thing, just a highly talented music major with a deep understanding of spiritual realities and an IQ probably north of 160."

Sarah smiled and grabbed at him playfully. "I see. That's the game, is it? This is what I get to look forward to for the rest of my life."

"That's right, sweetie, and that's a lot of potential to live up to!"

At least she had gotten Charlie laughing again.

chapter 45

"Bob, hi, it's Charlie Howell."

Charlie had wanted to wait a few days after the draft before calling Bob Neal. "Good to hear from you, Charlie. How's the leg?"

"No different. But that's not why I am calling."

"What's on your mind?"

"Looks like I might be in a situation similar to what you went through and was hoping you could share some of your thoughts with me."

"Sure. Anything in particular? I mean, if you are saying you have decided not to pursue baseball as a career, I think that's a little premature, Charlie. I think you should wait to see how you heal, maybe go through another draft next year."

"Well, I haven't really gotten to that point yet, but I do want to approach that decision-making process intelligently. I thought that given some of the things we discussed a couple of months ago and the way in which your own life unfolded, you might have some insights on how to deal with visions."

Peter A. Schuller

"Visions? Charlie, I am not a seer, just a psychologist."

"No, I don't mean that. I mean the ways in which one envisions his life unfolding—for example, I always saw myself as a shortstop, so that's where I played. I also always have known what kind of woman I would marry, how I would feel about my career, how I would balance my priorities. That sort of vision. Did that happen to you, and if so did your visions ever cause you to wonder about where they came from or what you should do about them?"

"Actually, you have come to the right source on that one, Charlie. I grew up with those types of visions and had to struggle with them for a number of years until I reconciled myself to what they were all about. I had always seen myself as a ballplayer, and that was a really difficult one to deal with. My wife and I also went through a rough patch, which did not at all accord with my vision of marriage, so I had to deal with that too. There are some other big ones as well, like my vision of what life would be like, how people would treat each other, and how much justice there would be in world."

"So what did you do?"

"I decided that I needed to treat my visions as sources of guidance, to honor them for their essence more than their content. In my younger years, I was sure that my vision for how things would be, or should be, reflected truths to pursue with unrelenting perseverance, until they materialized. I liked reading biographies, and it seemed as though great leaders shared one thing in common—they were visionaries and they never let go of their visions. They had visions about what they wanted to accomplish and where they wanted to take their followers. But over time, I realized that adopting this perspective also led many leaders to experience a great deal of angst too, especially when things didn't work out the way they had envisioned. There are certainly a lot of great leaders who have lived very difficult and emotionally trying lives. Once I realized that, the temptation was to see my visions as mere illusions, like the illusions we all build around we who are and how important we think we might be. In the last few years, however, I have been able to let go of that point of view too, in order to finally see my visions for life as guides. I see how they reflect what I stand for, what motivates me, what gives me a sense of integrity about my life."

"Interesting."

"Yeah, and shifting my perspective helped me adjust to some pervading disappointments as well."

"Such as?"

"Such as the notion that everyone understands fairness and aspires to create it. I have always had a strong sense of justice, and my vision of life was that as long as you sought fairness in all that you did, others would generally do so too. Baseball quickly disabused me of that vision—players using steroids, stealing signals, doctoring equipment—and obviously you don't have to look around too much to find that there are many people in this world who don't even understand fairness, let alone aspire to achieve it."

"And so how do you use visions as guides exactly?"

"Good question. For one, I let them inform my attitudes and keep me clear on what's important. I also let them remind me to live out my uniqueness, part of which is captured in my visions. Maybe my seeking and trying to do justice doesn't make much of a difference in the world, but it is important to my own sense of integrity, and the integrity with which I hope to live out my uniqueness. You certainly understand human uniqueness, Charlie, with all your work in neuroscience. Our hearts, souls, minds, whatever you want to call that dimension of human self, are as unique as our brains. I guess you might say that our souls are somehow embedded in the neurology of our brains. I don't know about that—I suppose it's possible—but there can't be much doubt about the fact that we are each unique in our approach to, and experience of, life. And we owe it to ourselves, even to life itself, to live out our uniqueness. On top of that, there was another aspect, an even more important one."

"Which was?"

"I am a little hesitant to get into this, Charlie. You know, preaching is not part of my professional activities, and it's not really within my personal comfort zone either."

"Consider it mentoring, then."

"Fair enough. Basically, I decided to set my priorities, to focus on the aspect of life that I felt was most important and let the other aspects take care of themselves. What I mean is, I decided to seek justice where I could, because I believe in God and it makes sense to me that the God of Creation is a God of Justice. In fact, the more I thought about justice in those terms, the more it seemed like the type of justice that I had always envisioned when I focused on pursuing fairness. Ironically, I have discovered that as long as I continue to seek justice, in the most divine sense of the word, I can let go of my frustration with the injustice and unfairness I encounter in daily life. Not that I quit seeking fairness—because being a person of integrity requires you to always seek out what you believe in, Charlie—but I just decided to quit letting all the unfairness get to me emotionally. I guess Buddhists would say I became more of a detached observer. Take you, for example. What happened to you was bloody unfair—a careless motorist, just before the draft. But it happened, Charlie, and much as I was disappointed, I accepted it, without much emotion. Don't get me wrong, I think it would be unrealistic for you to have quite the same point of view as I did. But you asked, so there it is."

"Thanks for sharing that, Bob. I actually have a vision about justice that sounds quite similar to yours, though I guess I have not spent enough time out in the 'real world' to have been become confused about it yet. What other types of notions have you been able to let go of exactly?"

"Well, for one thing, the idea that if you work hard and do the right thing, you will be fairly rewarded in life."

"You mean that isn't the way life is?!"

"No, Charlie, you will discover that life is not that way at all. Fairness, good fortune, and the reward for hard work are unevenly distributed in this world, and

I am sure I will never really understand why that is, but it seems as much a reality of life as anything I can think of."

"Honestly, that one will take a while for me to assimilate. Besides, I thought I remember your telling me just the other day that working hard is the key to success."

"It is, Charlie, but there is a big difference between being 'rewarded' and being 'successful'. The point I was trying to make earlier is that there is not always a direct causal link between hard work and how you may be rewarded for it. Over time, however, hard work will always bear fruit, even it is not the kind you might immediately consider an appropriate award for your work. Hard work will always eventually generate important new learning and growth, new insights and confidence, and ultimately the satisfaction of being able to say that whatever happened in your life, you lived it to the fullest. That, my friend, is the definition of success in my book."

"I see. That sounds pretty important. Would you mind writing that out for me in an email so I can read it again and fully absorb it?"

"Be happy to. That's what mentors are for."

"Thanks. I look forward to spending more time thinking about this, though the hard work bit I pretty much understand already. I can definitely do that."

"Good, and whatever you do, Charlie, just don't despair. Finding your way in the world, seeking justice, pursuing fairness *are* good and noble ways of being. The world needs more people with your vision, who have the courage and conviction to pursue it. But know that given the current state of humanity, such a journey won't be easy, and it may not have its manifest rewards.

"A life of sacrifice then?"

"Possibly. You are a gifted young man, Charlie, but that does not mean your life will be easy and rewarding, at least not in terms of the rewards most people seek. There is much more to life than playing baseball. But somehow I think you already knew that."

"Sarah and I have talked a lot about spiritual journey lately, but not about sacrifice. That's a more sobering subject it seems and a little harder for me to contemplate."

"Not unusual for a 21 year old."

"I suppose. But I really would be interested in talking to you more about that sometime."

"Sure. But don't stress about it now, Charlie. You have plenty of things to think about for the moment. Give me a call in a couple of weeks, after the whole post-draft madness has settled down."

"Thanks, I will."

"Good. I mean it. Call me."

chapter 46

WHEN CHARLIE KNOCKED, Sarah was sitting upright on her couch. She was consumed by a strange feeling, and she was not quite sure whether it was physical, emotional, or both. She could not help but think about her heart, having only been out of the hospital for a couple of weeks, but she thought it might have to do with her feelings for Charlie. She had felt so badly for Charlie during draft day, when he had to watch as his childhood dream seem to be slipping away, along with his innocence. Slowly, she rose from the couch and went to the door.

"Hi, Sarah. How are you?"

Sarah managed a weak smile, covering it with a lie. "Good, Charlie, and you?"

"Been down to the beach, just taking some time to think. There are a few things I would love to talk with you about. Had dinner yet?"

"No, I wasn't really hungry, so I was just about to have a yogurt. I was worried about you, wondering why you didn't call."

"Sorry. I guess I got a bit absorbed in my thoughts. But let me tell you what I discovered!"

Sarah wanted to shift her mood to match Charlie's enthusiasm but was finding it difficult. "Sure, Charlie, but not right now. Just sit here and hold me a moment."

"Of course. What's wrong? You don't look so well all of a sudden."

"I am not sure, Charlie. I have had this really strange feeling for the last 10 minutes."

"How about some tea? Maybe that will help."

"OK, but I can get it. Would you like some too?"

"Sure, thanks."

Sarah started to make her way to the kitchen but never made it.

Out of the corner of his eye, Charlie saw her collapse. She didn't stagger and fall. She dropped, like a stone. And as she did, Charlie's heart stopped. As he rushed to her side, he grabbed his cell phone out of his pocket and dialed 911.

Frantically, Charlie started administering what he hoped was proper CPR techniques, though he had never had any training. As the seconds passed, he realized how little he knew about the cardio pulmonary system and frantically hoped that the ambulance would arrive soon. What he did know was that after 10 seconds without blood, the brain began to die. Sarah was not breathing, and Charlie was overcome with the horror that she might already be gone. He refused to give up, but his brain was screaming in despair. Suddenly, he started to pray. He pleaded, he swore, he promised, and he pleaded some more. *Anything, God, anything.*

You can't let her go. She has too much to do. I need her. I promise to do whatever you want. Just don't let her go.

Ten minutes later, when the paramedics finally arrived, Sarah's face had completely lost its color. In a furious flurry of activity, they searched for a pulse, shoved an oxygen mask over her nose and mouth, and wrestled with the defibrillator. After several minutes they abruptly quit, and one of them slumped to the floor. In that moment, Charlie was overcome by a strange sensation and suddenly thought perhaps that he too might die. He even hoped for a second that he would. The emotional pain, if that is what it was, numbed not only his brain but his entire body. He had never known such limited consciousness in a wakened state. Then the thought came to him again that at that moment death might be a relief.

chapter 47

IN THE WEEKS after Sarah's death, Charlie was inconsolable. The existential cloud of hopelessness that he had occasionally experienced before Sarah died had grown into a full fledged depression. On a number of days, he just could not find anything worth living for, though he never really considered ending his life. And worst of all, he couldn't even conceive of how he would ever again feel happy or hopeful. The world as he knew it had disappeared. The world he lived in did not make sense any more.

He had spent a few days with Sarah's parents after the funeral, but they were so distraught that he sensed his presence was just making it more difficult for them. Ann Wilson had indeed become very fond of Charlie, and she was apparently grieving over not only having lost her daughter but the prospect of having Charlie slowly drift out of her life as well. Charlie had also spent a week with his own mother back in Maryland, and she had been wonderful in helping him with the grieving process, having been through it herself. She was strong and deeply compassionate, but even her love and affection were unable to shift Charlie's consciousness.

He had even tried to escape the pain by traveling, having been convinced by Russ that the two of them should just take off to Scotland for a week, but it didn't work. His leg was still bothering him, so he could not even enjoy the fabulous golf there, and even when he wasn't feeling emotionally numb, he still sensed he was wandering in a dark cloud that had no beginning or end. He had lost all of his visions for the future. Without a vision or sense of hope, how would one want to keep going? Didn't the brain *need* to have expectations and didn't the mind *need* to have hope?

After they returned from Scotland, Russ had moved back South, to a job in Atlanta with Coke, leaving Charlie alone for the first time since Sarah had died. He didn't know what he was going to do and had no idea where he wanted to live. He loved southern California, but there seemed to be too many memories there.

Finally, he called Bob Neal. After sharing some of his feelings and thoughts with his mentor, Bob was able to give Charlie something to hang onto, and it made sense.

"Charlie, the only thing you have to rely on here is process. The first part of the process involves the nurture of your soul. Your soul is on a journey, Charlie, and it does have guidance from a far more powerful intelligence than you and I can imagine. So get with someone who can help you through that part of the process, who can listen and guide you in a way that works for you. We all have our own ways of being and thinking, so make sure you find someone who can help you follow *yours*. The other part of the process is simpler—you just have to put yourself in play. You know, you can't win the lottery unless you buy a ticket, you can't steal home unless you get to third—you just have to get out there and start moving. Literally. The whole point is, and I know you appreciate this, you have to get your brain and body directed toward something. It's simply the nature of the human person—if we are not moving forward, we simply are not doing what we were made to do."

Charlie smiled to himself. "Yeah, Bob, I guess it's sort of like looking at humans as complex adaptive systems, which have to keep changing or face extinction."

"Precisely, Charlie. And I can tell you from personal experience that physically your body needs to keep moving and psychologically your mind needs to stage engaged, or you will start to wither. It's a very basic biochemical thing. You have way too much going for you to let that happen. So do me a favor, every morning you wake up, think of this conversation, make a pact to just do something that gets your body and mind moving that day, and dedicate your consciousness to just one thing—persevering. You may not be able to fathom it now, but things will change. You will emerge from this. Just persevere. You can do it, Charlie, and there are a lot of people who believe in you."

"Thanks, Bob. That does mean a lot to me. And I will think of you, and this conversation, when times are tough."

Soon thereafter, on a cool July morning, he found himself meandering down the beach at Crystal Cove, memories of Sarah flooding his consciousness. Tears began to stream down his face, but his body was moving, forward. He sensed Sarah's presence and suddenly a breath settled lightly on his spirit, filling his body in a way that he had never before experienced. The dark cloud that had covered his heart lifted, and for the first time since Sarah's death, he had a new vision. Instantly, he knew that vision would be enough for him, because in that moment he understood that rather than being lost to him, Sarah had emerged into the present and would forever remind him of how important it was to live, to keep moving forward.